FRANCES

DENYS VAL BAKER

WILLIAM KIMBER · LONDON

First published in 1985 by
WILLIAM KIMBER & CO. LIMITED
100 Jermyn Street, London SW1Y 6EE

© Estate of Denys Val Baker, 1985

ISBN 0 7183 0546 9

This is a revised edition of *The Widening Mirror*
published by Sampson, Low, Marston & Co in 1949.

Photoset in North Wales by
Derek Doyle & Associates Mold, Clwyd
and printed in Great Britain by
Biddles Limited, Guildford, Surrey

AUTHOR'S NOTE

The setting of this novel
is the immediate postwar period
in Britain.

I

That evening Frances was restless, and so was the farmhouse. A sour March wind came over the dark ridge of the Penwith Hills and fretted around the straw-thatched eaves and corners, wriggling under the oak beams and along the wide stone corridors and down the spiral staircase, puffing out candle flames, rattling the blue Minton plates and the shiny brass bowls that lined the huge hall dresser, shivering tiny whispers of unease among the neat and familiar furnishings. On its way the wind had stripped the bleak woods of their last coverings, whisking the dead leaves and dying undergrowth into strange formations whose meaning and purpose were not as before, and required new understanding.

The wind had been torn out of nowhere, to scurry across lands and seas until it was lost in the same vast and secretive womb from which it emerged: yet each moment of its journey was a direct influence, an irradicable memory, shaping the cosmic pattern far more subtly than through the physical revelation of a bent tree or a broken reed. The wind came in haste and vanished in a breathless echo, but as it hurried its shadow and its cold fingers through the cosy geography of the farmhouse there was an impression of a more lasting disturbance, almost as if the wind had lifted a secret trap-door or opened a window that had always been closed.

When she had put the children to bed Frances tiptoed down to the hallway and crouched in front of the great redbrick fireplace, warming her hands and her body in the smoking heat of a fire of pine logs. Although it was already dark outside she did not light the paraffin lamp, preferring the red glow with which the fire bathed the contours of the hall. She had always been secretly glad that the electricity company's efficient tentacles never reached as far as the farmhouse, even though the process of fetching and carrying paraffin, of filling and trimming lamps, involved so much extra time and trouble. A paraffin lamp seemed to fit in with the world of leaping fire flames and shadows dancing on the walls, of familiar surroundings softly outlined. It created no more than a gentle oasis of the artificial brightness belonging to man, enough for the human cultures of reading and writing and talking across a table, knitting needles and a patient chessboard; not enough to dispel the illusions of other worlds, imponderables, always sleeping in the shadows and the softly darkened corners.

Candles, the fire, the Aladdin lamp, not only gave cosiness but charged the long hallway with an air of mystery, a veneer of inexplicable history. The garish blaze of electric light bulbs would have stripped the shadows of their mystery, left the hallway ruthlessly exposed – a hollow room filled with furnishings. One felt that even the flames of the fire would, as their rich colour faded by comparison, have shrunk into a more austere, non-committal warmth, as of the super-flat's gilded electric stove.

And yet it was that very simile, reversed, that was occurring to Frances now as she stood up abruptly and leaned on the mantelpiece, one white finger tracing the circle of the clock, her eyes watching a spark of wood burning in the grate, her head bowed with the weight of its thoughts. What if by living constantly in a half-lit world, something escaped, hidden away in the shadows? Something that was imperative to life, as much as an arm or a leg, without which there was no wholeness? Was not it time then to seek the surgeon-like decision of the electric light, to expose everything and perhaps understand what was there, needed?

Another evening she would have taken a book and sat curled up on the wide plush settee, the two or three hours slipping by comfortably until the high-pitched whine of the Lagonda coming up the lane awoke her to reality and her husband's return from his meeting in Bedruthan. But tonight she found it

impossible to relax, disturbed by one small thing after another
– an eerie owl hoot, a shower of sparks from the fire, then the
insolent caperings of the wind, ruffling the silence her
tenseness craved. She cultivated a resentment against the wind,
walking about as if trying to combat its intrusion, making sure
windows were closed, doors on the latch, investigating the
most minute sources of rattling. She lit a candle and went into
the dining-room, its atmosphere still faintly coloured with the
sweet smells and sticky echoes of the children's exuberant
teatime. The curtains were rustled slightly. She drew them over
carefully, shutting out the billowing darkness, encasing herself
in this dark oak-panelled room that time had fashioned into
an intimate property of her life.

The table-cloth had been left on and places laid for three.
When Oliver came in she would call up to Raymond, working
in his remote attic room, and the three of them would sit
round to a meal of cold ham and salad, thick slabs of
home-made bread and cheese and a pot of strong tea. She
smiled at her sentimentality, the fleeting vision of the cosy
family circle, herself in the end seat, her husband at one side
and her brother opposite, the children asleep upstairs; the
wanderers home and all's well.

Something made her sigh, and because she did not quite
know why she felt a sudden irritability and walked quickly out
of the room. The smile on her face became fixed, like a mask,
so that she, still a beautiful woman at thirty-five, took on an
unfamiliar agedness. As she went by the hall mirror she caught
a glimpse of her face, pale and strained in the candlelight, and
momentarily she fancied she was looking at the face of another
woman. Examining the reflection critically, she knew that what
she saw was not so much a reflection as an image. The beauty
could be titivated and recaptured, indeed: but the image
remained, some stranger who would not depart nor yet
introduce herself.

It was, she hazarded a guess – crossing the hall and
investigating into the library where a window had blown open
and was creaking backwards and forwards – the image
produced by super-imposing one face, or one expression,

upon another. There was, first, the face that was over-familiar, a face of considerable beauty deriving no little from a sort of inward serenity and contentment, the face of Mrs Frances Williams, the wife of Oliver Williams, the mother of Timothy and Theresa Williams, and the mistress of Tregonna Farm. And there was another face that was becoming almost as familiar to her, the face of Frances, the woman, untrammelled by any of these external if realistic trappings, isolated and momentarily excused from all obligation to others. She was able to convince herself of her intimate knowledge and complete understanding of both these faces. What remained incomprehensible and therefore frightening was the misty, undefined face that was produced by the fusion of the two reflections so familiar. That this should so completely elude her grasp was the most disturbing prospect of all since she knew, already, that it contained the revelation of her immediate and inescapable future.

The window closed, she turned and held the candle above her head so that its thin yellow tongue flickered life into the neat rows of books, the two polished writing-desks, the squat Belgian fire-stove which stood where one expected an open fireplace, adding its touch of originality to the scene. She walked over to the bookshelves and trailed her fingers lightly along the books. She liked to feel the smooth glossy spines, each one symbol of so much intangible reality. There were hundreds of books in this room; many of them were here when she came, relic of some stranger's life long ago closed. To them, over the ten years, she had added her own slow accumulation of coloured novels and slim poetry volumes. In one corner Oliver's farming books had formed themselves into a neat, rather forbidding pillar, beneath them the yellow and green files of the *Farmer's Weekly* and the *Farmer and Stockbreeder*. Then Raymond's arrival had quickly swollen the mole-hill into a mountain with his haphazard armfuls of books of all shapes and sizes.

Her eyes softened as she thought of Raymond, remote in the long bare attic, sitting before his elderly battered typewriter and hacking on to the paper the myths and fantasies of his life, or she hoped so, and that he wasn't sitting and drinking, instead. She looked around the library again with a new warmth. It occurred to her that although there was an intimacy between herself and every room in the house, in each case the intimacy was shared with a different person. When she thought of the dining-room she saw at once the twin, dark tousled heads of Timothy and Theresa, their guileless faces peeping over the table cloth, slightly stained and flushed from meals only too avariciously enjoyed. Timothy with his slightly rounder, more humorous face, Theresa with her precise, graver features that always seemed overclouded with some brooding conflict: twins of the same dark beauty yet, subtly, professing such different destinies.

The dining-room was hers and theirs almost entirely, so often were Oliver and Raymond away or working. At most meals there were just the three of them, and these were times of shrill torrents of patternless but delightful conversation. It was the dining-room, too, where on the wet, hopeless days, the twins were left to play and make their explorations with books and games and self-created fantasies.

Likewise, when she thought of the kitchen she was reminded always of herself and Edith, the plump, unabashed gossiper from the village, who struggled the two miles every day, often through slush and mud, and who she sometimes saw as the one pillar on which the house and they leaned, without which they would collapse into chaos.

And so, when she thought of the library she could only do so in association with her brother. She could, indeed, hardly visualise the room without her brother's presence, remembering those placid afternoons, when the children were at school and she sat at the window seat while Raymond pottered about the room, taking down a book and becoming lost into its world for half an hour – or sitting at the desk and scribbling furiously, tearing sheet after sheet from the neat white pad and piling them around him like frothing waves. She was always aware of being happy then, partly because of her own sense of relaxation, but more, because of the knowledge that here, at least, Raymond seemed at peace – here, momentarily, there was a lifting of the painful weight of inner turmoil which his very presence seemed to thrust forward hopelessly, accusingly.

They seldom spoke during those afternoons; there was no need to. She was always conscious of an immense bond of sympathy, an intuitive understanding between them – a closeness that nowadays she found it difficult to achieve elsewhere. Yes, Raymond and she belonged to the library – perhaps, also, to the attic, but then she hardly remembered when she had last penetrated into the attic. She had always assumed that it was his jealously guarded last retreat. She frowned thoughtfully. Perhaps she was wrong to assume that, perhaps in his loneliness he needed her more than before? And she sighed again, wishing that there was no problem greater than Raymond, or that he was not her problem at all.

In the hall again she stood irresolute, wondering whether it was merely her own imagination or whether the house really was possessed this evening by some extra unrest so that lights and shadows merged into grotesque beckoning shapes and the air was alive with the sound of rattling window panes and fumbling doors. She cupped one hand around the candle light to guard it from unheralded flickers of wind, and mounted the stairways.

Halfway up, where the stairs took a right-angled bend, she passed a tall gilt-framed mirror. When they came to the house, the mirror was tucked away in a loft and in its place hung a huge faded oil painting of one of the earliest owners of the house, a sad-looking major of the Balaclavas who had fought gallantly at the battle of Waterloo and who, local legend avowed, had drowned himself after the death of his wife.

The painting had always fascinated Frances. Every time she walked up or down the stairs or across the hallway – almost, she sometimes felt, as soon as she entered the front doorway – she had been conscious of this strange, far removed man looking down upon her, observing her every movement through the dust-rimmed metallic glance of his eyes. At first she had felt nervous, afraid that the eyes viewed her disapprovingly, seeing her as some intruder, hateful claimant to the place and atmosphere whose tradition belonged to a secure past. But one day, quite suddenly, she had realised that instead of disapproval the eyes revealed a wistful, rather charming welcome. She had felt that in some intangible way she had been accepted into the house, almost as into a family, and the knowledge had made her extraordinarily happy. She had smiled at the immobile major, as she might have smiled at some charming suitor, and it had not seemed entirely her imagination that the cold brown eyes momentarily softened and lit up in the warm glow, of her own look.

After that she had grown used to the picture, until it was a recognised, familiar part of her everyday life, like another relative. It had been quite a shock to her, coming in from a trip to the village one afternoon, to find the picture removed, its place filled by the tall, rather cold gilt mirror. Oliver had taken the picture away. It was a ridiculous piece of antiquity, he said, and had no part in their life. And he couldn't stand another minute of living under the gaze of a military blimp. When she had tried awkwardly to explain what the picture had represented to her he had looked at her at first angrily, and then pityingly, as if she were a child, and she had stopped in the middle of a sentence, feeling the futility of going on. Oliver had had his way.

And this, this was the room that could belong only to her and Oliver, she thought, pausing at the wide doorway of their bedroom and holding the candle light high above her head so that it cast its light across the green carpet and the oval dressing table, the marble washstand and the big white chest of drawers, to the wide double-poster bed that stretched along the further wall. It was a cosy room, with oak panelled walls and a low white ceiling, and the fire she had lit earlier in the evening was burning up brightly. It was a room in which, once she had shut the door behind her, she felt herself immersed into a small separate world that extended no further. Its geography was a country of satin dresses and cotton frills and a high necked purple dressing gown, some old silver slippers, a box of trinkets, the silver-plated brush which she used every night to brush back her long black hair – but also a country of brown leggings and hobbled boots, neatly folded corduroy trousers, a polo sweater, a black leather windjammer jacket, the conventional striped pyjamas. Its history was subtly present, yet hidden, veiled behind lace curtains, dancing in the fire flames of a hundred evenings, gently written across the smooth glossy old bedcover, the generous deep arms of the armchair; peeping around the corners of the dressing-table mirror.

It was a room impregnated, as intensely and yet diffusely as she was, by Oliver. She felt his presence everywhere, even though he was not there but miles away racing across the lonely moor road. It was not a presence that could be pushed away, forgotten, into a corner, or tucked into a drawer. There was something resilient about it, formidable and even aggressive. She had not been so conscious of this in the early years of their marriage, but the conviction had grown upon her lately. Even now when his presence was a sensation rather than a physical thing she could almost feel it impinging upon herself, some alien will endeavouring to force itself upon her, in some subtle way to direct her thoughts and her feelings – just as, she had become convinced, Oliver's natural reaction was to tend to dominate, to direct. And yet. There was something always comforting in strength, even if misused. She could feel herself opening towards it even now, gaining a strange sort of nourishment from this atmosphere of Oliver, Oliver, Oliver.

It would be difficult, she reflected, for many women to have resisted the sheer fascination of being carried along on the steady wave of Oliver's unshakable self-assurance, so persuasive in its utter certainty. For years that was exactly what she had done, for years her whole life, she now realised, had bloomed out on a pattern – a rich, rather beautiful pattern – but one that rested always on the solid foundation of Oliver's dominance, Oliver's ultimate authority. And the key to it all, the lubrication, she supposed, had been Oliver's sense of purpose; that was the cool, self-possessed instrument with which their lives had fashioned a future.

Paradoxically, it was that very thing that she most of all admired in Oliver, the utter ruthlessness with which he applied himself to achieving those things which he set his heart on –

including herself. There was something rather exquisite, she remembered even after ten years, in being made the focus of a strong man's ambition. Even now, at the memory, she felt a gentle tongue of colour wander over her cheeks, and she raised her fingers to feel the warm blood. But in a few moments the blood subsided, and her fingers grew cold. Ten years is a long time, she thought, and I am ten years older and wiser than I was, and the ten years are unalterable and immovable and part of eternity, the pattern irretraceable – but, she thought, the next ten years or the next five years, or the next year, are imponderable and uncharted. And as she fell into that reverie that had become so common to her lately, a sort of prodding self-exploratory study of herself, she felt Oliver's presence no longer as sustenance, but intrusion.

She shook her shoulders almost in irritation, and went over to the windows to stare out into the equally imponderable night. For it had become like that, lately, she knew. Within her, somehow, there had grown up another inner strength so that she no longer needed, and soon perhaps would not be able to bear, always to be supported on Oliver's self-assurance.

Sometimes she felt her thoughts almost clarified into the point of falling into neat places to form the picture that would explain all the confusions that filled her mind – that evening, she felt for a moment that she suddenly saw everything quite clearly. It was not, she felt yet again, that she was out of love with Oliver. It was that she was not as she had been, and the balance must be adjusted.

The problem, she thought with a sigh, was really Oliver's. But that he was unlikely to realise, she imagined; and her long, pale face grew cold and rather sad as she sat and stared out on the dull shapes of the farm and the out-houses, the long cowshed and the crumbling barn where the oats were stored, in the distance the unexpected flicker of light from the little wood-shed in the middle field where Mark, the former German prisoner who had stayed on as their farmhand, would be warming himself by a tiny Valor stove before going to sleep – until at long last she heard the whine of the Lagonda from far away, and the beaming lights broke over the hill top and rushed up the winding mud lane.

*

'What about a glass of sherry?' said Oliver. He was in an excellent humour, his face flushed, his eyes bright and mischievous. All through dinner he had delighted in elaborating a sardonic account of the meeting of the local National Farmers' Union which they had attended earlier in the evening.

'Excellent idea. I should think we've earned it.' Raymond sprawled himself across his favourite armchair, one leg dangling idly over the side. 'My God, the petty childish things that excite these stolid hearty neighbours of ours.' He deepened his voice, gutturally mimicking. 'Mr Penna's gate has had the lock damaged. Mr Hosking hasn't had his fair share of the agricultural subsidies. Mr Bennett's cows have broken down Mr Pengelly's new bamboo fence – says Mr Pengelly. Stop Press. Mr Pengelly's horse has eaten part of Mr Bennett's new cut oats – says Mr Bennett. Why, they get so emotional about it you can see the veins standing out in their necks. I swear sometimes that old Forster, who's about the biggest crook in the district, is near to tears.'

'Well, I think it's good that they do show emotion,' said Frances placidly. 'At least they have some feelings.'

'Oh yes,' said Raymond sarcastically. '*Some* feelings for *some* things. Never the right feelings for the right things. What do they care about the things that really matter? Look how they're up in arms at the slightest move to pay higher wages, or to look after their workers. And what do they care about what goes on outside their own little petty world of crops and markets and – and prize pigs!'

Frances smiled indulgently.

'Aren't you lumping them all together in one mouldy heap, darling? There are good farmers as well as bad ones.'

'Yes, yes, of course.' As always in any discussion, Raymond's unnatural tautness evinced itself. His high-boned face seemed to tighten, his voice harshened and he spoke with almost painful intensity. There was a thin weal along one side of his forehead, where a bullet had grazed him in the fighting at Caen during the war. At any excitement it reddened and seemed to protrude, adding to the twisted, rather embittered look of his face.

'There *are* good farmers – Oliver is an example. Oh, I don't say that because he's Oliver – it's what anyone round here would admit. He pays workers a fair wage, he doesn't let the farm go to rack and ruin, he doesn't try to swindle on deals, he –'

'Here, I say,' interposed Oliver protestingly, 'another glass of sherry and you'll be giving me a halo.'

He smiled, all the same, never able not to enjoy praise. And after all he knew that he was a good farmer. He knew that he would have made a good job of whatever he had done – whether it was farming or engineering or even banking. He had known that as long as he could remember, from those earliest childhood times when he had found how simple it was always to get his own way if he set his mind hard enough on it. It was as if there had been born in him a seemingly effortless flair for achievement – so that he was a good footballer, a good cricketer, a fine mathematician, a most competent woodworker. When he took up driving, he drove extremely well, if rather recklessly. He often wished that he had made a profession of motor-racing; there was something fascinating and challenging to him about speed; possibly, he sometimes thought, because its challenge was infinite – there would never be an end or a limit to the possible achievement, you strained further and further.

There had been the same attraction about his farming. In four years he had built up a semi-derelict farm that was once half under water and made it an extremely profitable business. Of course, it had been easier for him being born of the country, reared in the country. It had been in his bones, the few years in between working in London on his uncle's motor car firm had been merely an interlude, all the time he had remained at heart in his native Cornwall – when his father died it had been inevitable that he should use the money to

re-install his roots in the country. It had been fortunate that
Frances had shared this desire – not that he wouldn't have
somehow persuaded her.

Yet it might have been difficult. His eyes slanted sideways,
studying her face, cupped in one hand as she looked across at
Raymond. He saw not what someone else, a stranger, would
have seen, something lovely yet on the surface – but what only
he could have seen, with the deep intimacy of their knowledge
of each other. And yet, even with that, you could never be sure.
You could never be sure what people were really thinking,
feeling. What was she thinking *now*?

'Penny for them, Frances?'

He stretched a hand over and touched her lightly on the
wrist. She started.

'Oh … Nothing, nothing. I was – thinking about what
Raymond was saying. That's all.'

Obviously that wasn't all. Oliver sighed. He always felt
disgruntled at the thought of other worlds, with which he was
not familiar, occupying the attention of those near to him.

'Well, Raymond and I have done enough talking.' He
laughed suddenly. He was in any case feeling pleased with life.
He had scored quite a debating success at the meeting. There
was no reason not to feel happy, continue to feel happy.

'Truth to tell, we had one or two drinks before we started
off, didn't we, Ray? That's what's really made us so talkative …
But what about you. Any news? The children go to bed all
right? What do they think of being on holiday?'

Frances smiled, her face breaking alive.

'They're basking in it. Timothy's absolutely mad about the
box of tools you gave him. He spent hours today hacking away
at a revolting piece of wood and in the end produced what he
gravely called a racing motor. Edith wanted to put it on the fire
– you should have seen Timothy's face!'

Frances laughed at the memory. Oliver joined in, easily,
light-heartedly. Raymond's mirth was quieter, a quick nervous
smile while his eyes flitted affectionately from one to the other.
He experienced a moment of peace. They were rare moments
in his life, it seemed, and they usually occurred here, the three

of them sitting round the table. Perhaps it was that they all played their parts correctly, so that here was only one world, a light, happy world, food on the table, drink in the glasses, the lights soft, the fire warm and sleepy. He could be happy, always, he sometimes felt, just sitting here, the three of them, not moving, never moving. But he knew life, at least his life, like a pattern, ice-clear. Stay a moment too long, cling a moment further, and not only the moment would be spoilt – there would never be any more.

But tonight there was time yet to linger. He offered Frances a cigarette as she and Oliver came and sat on the couch. It was probably her second or third of the day. It was his thirtieth. That was the real difference between them, the only one. They had almost the same tastes, it was just that he plunged to the excesses, Frances – Frances was always well in control. He smiled to himself. There was more to it than that – what he meant was that Frances had the strength to control the stupid excesses, he hadn't. He thought of his gramophone case in his room, where he kept the hoarded bottle of gin – there was only a tiny drop left in one, he knew, and that would have to suffice. God, what a pity he hadn't got Frances' control.

And yet – he looked at her thoughtfully, through the ringed centre of a puff of cigarette smoke – he was sure Frances was capable of excesses in the sensible sort of things. There was a warmth and sensuousness about her that would have made it impossible for her not to do so. He remembered her anguish over a fox that had been badly mauled by the hounds, how her whole being had seemed to give out to it, loving it, caring for it, healing it. Damn the fox, that hardly mattered, but there was something wonderfully right about Frances' unhesitating excess. Then there was the way she could go into raptures about some new scheme of decorating the house, or about embarking on some treat with the children. And then – he looked at her slyly again, noting the strong, rounded lines, the soft desirability that seemed to nestle around her like a frothy cloak. She would be a good lover, there would be no life-denying control there, she would give herself liberally and warmly, and that would be good, too.

He looked at Oliver. Oliver was a lucky man. Sometimes when he looked at Oliver, and then at Frances, he thought he had never seen two such dissimilar people. Some strange sense of discretion had kept him from ever voicing this opinion, but he often wondered whether it had ever occurred to either of them. Perhaps never to Oliver, that wasn't the way his mind would work. But Frances, surely? He looked at her face, and away again. Inscrutable Frances. As all women, inscrutable. You never really knew them. He didn't suppose, really, that Oliver knew Frances – perhaps, in some odd way, he knew Frances better himself.

There were things that brothers and sisters knew in their blood and bones, that never had to be expressed, that even lovers would not understand to the same degree. As if in some peculiar way brothers and sisters were tuned in on a particular wave-length. As now – he had only to clear his mind of other things, of futile disturbances about NFU hypocrisy and stupid regrets for gin that wasn't there, and he could tune in to Frances, he could know exactly what sort of mood she was in. And there you were, why dammit, he could feel it – a sort of restlessness, quite a turmoil of restlessness, that belied the placid look and calmness in her face. He watched her closely, wondering what it was, knowing that it must be something outside their world else she would have come and talked to him.

At the thought his heart ached to be able to help her, he was conscious as always of the enormous love which he bore for her – the one pure unselfish thing in his life he felt, removed from the jungles of other human relationships with all their complexities of desire and possessiveness. He longed to be able to stretch a hand out and smooth her hair back, as he used to do when they were children. He wanted her to know that he sensed her mood, that he understood the mood if not its detail. He knew that, in an odd way, the knowledge would comfort her.

And because there was no way of doing it directly he fell to staring into the fire and thinking, while Oliver talked mildly about farming matters. Suddenly Raymond leaped to his feet in that abrupt, almost inhuman way that marked him off the average, that always made companions a trifle uneasy, never quite sure whether they were in the presence of someone quite normal.

'Going already?' said Oliver in surprise.

'No ... not at once. Just going to get a book.'

He hurried into the library, struck a match and went almost without hesitation to the book he wanted.

'Frances,' he said, coming back to the hallway. 'Can I just read you a passage? Do you mind, Oliver? It won't take long.'

'Of course not. What will it be?'

Raymond fingered among the pages nervously, his tongue running over the tip of his lips until he had found what he was looking for.

'Ah, here it is ... It's a little piece by Yeats.'

And he began reading, quickly, a trifle breathlessly, in clear, musical tones that echoed sweetly about the warm fire-splayed room, seeming to match the rich warmth of the oak walls and the cream carpet, the close cosiness of the candlelights ...

'That's all.'

Raymond's voice was suddenly flat and tired, a stranger to the voice that had vibrated with life as it read the poem. Closing the book with a snap he put it on top of the burnt-edged mantelpiece beam and stood staring into the fire. Deep in the flames he fancied he could seek the lurking contentment that always seemed to elude his grasp. Sometimes he thought he had captured it – when he was lost in the magic of a beautiful poem or caught up in an exhilarating whirl of his own writing, words taking possession of him in an erotic ecstasy. But if so, it was lost as soon as it was gained; there remained only a sense of deflation; after the wonder only the echo.

'Thank you, Raymond.'

Frances' voice came over his shoulder, familiar whisper in the night that had so often comforted him in the past. He knew without turning, from the very inflection, that she was thanking him for having felt her unhappiness, for having tried to share it. Why could he not be satisfied at that, he reflected, watching one long blue spike of flame whip in a savage spiral towards its own eternity. But he wasn't, he couldn't be, he always wanted something more. Even now there was part of him deep down that wanted not only her appreciation, not only her understanding, but also her sympathy. At that moment, kicking miserably at a crumbling wood log, he hated himself because he thought he saw his true nature, always demanding, demanding, demanding to be comforted. And because he knew that he had not the strength to stay and be silent, that he could only avoid the problem by forcing himself to go.

'I think I'll go up now ... perhaps do a spot of writing.' He turned from the fire, clasping his hands behind him.

'I'm glad you like it, Frances,' he muttered. 'If you want to read it again, I've marked the place.' He bent stiffly and kissed the top of her forehead. 'Good night. Good night, Oliver.'

'Good night, Ray.'

They watched him go in silence, the tall spare figure crossing the wide hallway and leaving a reed-like shadow that vanished as soon as he mounted the stairs. He saw them watching him, in the mirror, and the sense of their separateness filled him with a loneliness that hung like a stone around his heart all the long winding way to his attic.

Frances sighed.

Oliver smiled faintly.

'Don't worry, old girl. Ray's often quite happy when he seems extremely miserable. He quite enjoyed tonight, you know. Especially having something he could pull to pieces later. I wish I had his gift for pointed invective.'

Seeing Oliver's frown, a trifle portentous, Frances felt a ripple of affection.

'You are a funny thing. You'd certainly be a poor hand at invective. You're far too sentimental, for one thing.'

'Sentimental?' Oliver considered his own conception of sentimentality: fussing about animals, weeping over slushy novels, sugary memories of the past. These were none of his weaknesses. 'I'd hardly call myself that.'

'No?' Frances stared at him thoughtfully. The affection that had rushed up so unexpectedly, already was flooding away. It could not by its careless visit uproot the strange resentment that had grown so slowly and ominously in recent weeks. And now it irked her immediately that Oliver should always seem to oppose any suggestion of hers, even on such a superficial point.

'All right, then. You're not sentimental. You're just and considerate, and you don't stand for any nonsense. There, is that what you wanted me to say?'

Despite herself her voice trembled. Annoyed that she should be so easily provoked, she got up and went across to the sideboard, picked out an apple and began peeling it, to keep her hands and her mind occupied.

Oliver shrugged.

'Sorry.'

Frances came back, threw the peel into the fire. All that evening she had felt the restlessness growing and feeding within her, like elements gathering for a storm. Yet she hardly knew what it was she would say, even if she wanted to make some eventful statement. She looked down at Oliver's face, slightly averted, round and full-fleshed, a little pink from the fire, the eyes well-set and strong, now gazing, a little lost, at the pattern of the rug. He was probably sulking a little. There was always that lurking touch of the child in him, beneath the impressive exterior. It was in every man she supposed, and part of what women loved them for. But tonight it seemed to her merely as irritating as the argumentativeness, the domination. Tonight she had an immense desire to be acknowledged as an equal, a separate human being.

She wondered if she could explain this, in some way.

'Oliver.'

She hesitated.

'Yes?'

'Oliver, I've been wondering ...'

He looked up from the carpet. But his eyes were careful, guarded. He was on the defensive. She sighed.

'Oh, it doesn't matter. Nothing.'

She came and sat beside him. They were good friends,

companions in so much. That was a separate, unbreakable thing.

'Tell me things.'

He frowned, still acting resistance.

'What things?'

She pouted, and nestled down into the couch, one arm lying along the back.

'Don't be silly, darling. About the farm. Plans. What did Dakers say about your idea for co-operative marketing?'

'Oh ... that.' Oliver managed to impart all the characteristics of boredom and nonchalance to the word. But it was impossible for him to remain long withdrawn. He thawed easily. For him problems always vanished. He grinned.

'Well, tell you the truth, Dakers said quite a lot. He seems to think it's an excellent idea. In fact, he and I are going to ...'

Frances listened, her eyes gently half-closed, listened to the eager words pouring out, the stream of those material events which was so much their life. Progress, progress, progress – there was always progress with Oliver. Things did not stand still, his ambition was unquenchable, would always carry them forward into a never unexciting future. Tonight, as ever, there was a strange comfort to listen, to have it handed to one on a plate, to know this would be and that would be. And yet – and yet tonight it was not enough. But it was at least peaceful for a while to let Oliver talk, while she tried to collect her strange, unhappy thoughts.

*

Upstairs, in the familiar blue room, by the fitful light of the dying fire, they undressed in silence. She took off her clothes in one continuous movement, throwing them carelessly to one side and jumping quickly in between the sheets. Oliver undressed more slowly, more precisely, folding each garment and draping it neatly on the back of a chair. He drew the curtains and opened one of the windows, letting in a sweet rush of fresh evening air. Then he got in beside her quietly. She felt him stretching out his limbs with the luxurious complacence of one who was pleased with his day's work. She could feel the warmth of his closeness to her, the familiar smell of him; deep down the stir of excitement.

'Darling,' he whispered. 'Frances, darling …'

'No!' she said, almost angrily, and with a swift movement she turned her back on him, away to the silver-rimmed duskiness of the night outside.

For a long time, long after he had fallen into what she supposed was an embittered sleep, she lay staring out of the window. Once she raised herself on one elbow and saw that the tiny light of Mark's hut was still winking away, like yet another star. When she lay back she carried its image with her, thinking of that other solitary man who sat so alone in the night, wondering what were his thoughts, wondering what had been his life, wondering what would be his dreams when finally he slept. And she was aware not so much of pity, though there was that, as of having acquired a new layer of understanding – of how immensely alone in the world, at root, was every human being, and of the impossibility of it ever being otherwise. And perhaps that in the forlorn attempt to challenge this loneliness lay the whole secret of life.

II

Timothy yawned and stared at the bottom of the bed where he was making his two big toes bob up and down under the bed-clothes, like the humps of a camel. When he was tired of this pastime he looked across at the bed on the other side of the room, at the crumpled and apparently inanimate mess of bedclothes that contained his sister.

'Terra.'

The bedclothes gave the tiniest stir of movement.

'Terra!'

'Mmmmhh?'

'What day is it?'

'Mmmmhhh – Friday, I think.'

'The day Daddy drives to Bedruthan?'

'No, that's Saturday, you silly. Shut up, Timothy, I'm not properly awake yet.'

'I am. Wide awake.'

He stared around at the white clarity of the room, enumerating the familiar landmarks: the green chest of drawers with the broken leg, the mirror with the long crack down it where he had thrown a marble at it, the squat portmanteau, the tiny table in the corner piled high with parts and remnants and even whole pieces of toys and gadgets, mostly his. The huge coloured map which Oliver had pinned up along most of one wall, and which neither of them could understand. A pile of silly girls' books that Terra was always reading, with gold and red painted covers. A rusty bucket which they took down to the river when they went exploring. A funny picture of a big fat man slipping on a banana skin that

Aunty Edie had given them at Christmas. And, on the top of the chest of drawers, in pride of place, a bright shiny mechanical motorboat, a creation of Oliver's out of old pieces of tin scrap. It looked terribly exciting, all they needed now was a key to wind it, and then they could go and try it out on the cow's pond.

He screwed up his round, bright-rimmed eyes.

'Terra, the sun's awfully bright. I'm sure it's terribly late.'

'Mmmmmh.'

'Besides, I can hear Uncle Raymond getting up. It must be quite late, really.'

'Perhaps he's helping mother.'

'Even so, it must be quite late.'

'Oh, Timothy! Be quiet.'

He pouted, resting his chin on the bedclothes.

'We've been in bed for hours and hours and hours.'

He relapsed into a temporary, moody silence. Outside he could hear the trills and warbles of birds, an occasional far off bleat from a sheep, the strange untraceable sounds that might be something exciting. He was glad the school holidays were still on, excusing him the walk up the hill into the village, the long dull hours listening to Miss Penberthy. Instead, the whole (free) day of freedom lay before them, to do with what they liked. His eyes gleamed excitedly as a hundred and one possibilities jumped into his mind.

'Terra, let's get up soon. Then, after breakfast, let's get Uncle Raymond to take us to the reservoir.' That would be fun: Uncle Raymond played all sorts of games with them, battles and ambushes, and he swore at them just like a real soldier. The idea captured his imagination wholly, and with a tingle of pleasure he jumped out of bed and ran across to his sister's bed.

'Do let's, Terra. Such fun.' Oh, come on, he thought, looking disgruntledly at the shapeless mound. Girls were lazy. Staying in bed all the time. Suddenly his patience completely evaporated.

'Lazy Lizzy!' he called out disparagingly, and he began tugging the bedclothes away.

'Timothy – Timothy! Oh, you beast. Beee-ast!'

The last epithet was dragged out into a despairing wail as two small but determined hands tugged the last of the bedclothes away and bared the curled cosy figure of Theresa to the embrace of the morning air. With her long black hair coiling all over her shoulders, scrawny across her face, she looked like a ruffled kitten. And like a kitten she opened first one bright black eye, then another, peeping through strands of overhanging hair as if still half hoping that what seemed to be was merely part of a dream.

At last, seeing that it wasn't, she uncurled and sat up on the edge of her bed, wriggling into the warmth of a dressing gown.

'Just you wait, Timothy! Just you wait!'

And then, with the grim purpose of any rudely awakened sleeper, she began chasing her grinning brother around the room.

'You wait!'

'Ha! Ha! Lazy Lizzie!'

'You –'

They jumped over one bed, encircled the table, navigated two dangerous corners. A few toys were scattered in many directions. Two of the heaviest books tumbled off the drawers. The floor reverberated with the swift footsteps of the hunted and the hunter.

'Terra's out of be-ed! Terra's out of be-ed!'

She brushed the coils back over her shoulders and made a swift leap forward. He scrambled, giggling with the nervous anticipatory laughter of a cornered prey.

'Now, you wait. I'll tickle your sides, and the soles of your feet. And I'll twist your nose, I will!'

They fell, a muddle of threshing limbs, upon Timothy's bed. Their high-pitched screams of laughter, their blood-curdling threats, rose high into the morning air. Under their weight the bed sagged and groaned alarmingly. Elbows, kneecaps, even heads as well as the heavy brass ends of the bed, banged in rapid succession against the two corner walls, like the drums of doom.

When, finally exhausted, they lay panting on the bed they

did not move for a while, enjoying another half-giggly respite before the energetic course of their day began. Then, hearing the grandfather clock striking eight o'clock, they shouted out in dismay and hurled themselves into movement. They had work, duties, tasks, all important, to execute before they could with any conscience present themselves at the breakfast table; Theresa's the job of feeding the two rabbits, the two love-birds, Hamish the tortoise (if he could be found); Timothy's the mission of touring the out-houses, inspecting the horses, the cows, the pigs and the poultry, satisfying himself with grave knowing nods as to their general good health and happiness (they would of course have been fed an hour earlier by the diligent Mr Bailey, the cowman). Life, even on holiday, had its immense purpose and programmes.

*

After breakfast Oliver put on his brown gaiters, picked up the white stick he always carried with him, and went out into the rickyard. He usually sat on for a while after breakfast, smoking a pipe, reading a book, or talking to Frances and the children. But this morning he had felt ill at ease. There had been conversation yet it had the hollow echo of formality; underneath it lurked a wisplike tension that he could not define, but of which he was subtly aware.

Though he had slept reasonably well he had awoken several times. Once he had opened his eyes to see Frances sitting up in bed, her head turned toward the window so that her profile was caught in a moonglowed silhouette – looking, it seemed to him in the half-awake world of the night, like a marble statue. The conception of her as frozen into an immobile shape had lingered with him, hauntingly, in some way carrying into the morning life and inhibiting him so that he was himself reticent and shy of conversation. He had been glad to gulp down the food, to ruffle the children's hair and go out of the room without directly looking at Frances.

Out in the yard his eyes examined the familiar items; the two ricks, the tractor in the shed, the padlocked stable doors, the heap of potash, the pile of new hay for the pigsties, wood logs to be chopped for the evening fires. There was nothing for him to do here. The day's programme would be the hard routine one, ploughing the north field as soon as Bailey arrived back with the mended plough. Until then his time was free. He decided it would be best expended upon a tour of the farm's fences. Besides, a long brisk walk in the fresh September air would do him good.

He hesitated, aware somehow of a sense of loneliness. Making up his mind he went across to the door of the cowshed.

'Mark – I want you to come with me a while.'

Mark came out, pulling down his shirt-sleeves over narrow white forearms. He was tall and thin, with hair that was almost white, cropped short and brushed back over a wide brow. He had the high-boned, slightly hollow face of an intellectual, normally rather pallid but now tanned a deep brown from a whole summer working in the fields. His eyes were a soft grey, his mouth small and delicately curved, almost like a woman's.

'I thought we'd take a look at the fences,' said Oliver. 'Bring a billhook with you and we can do a bit of trimming as we go along.'

Mark nodded. He had never wanted to be a part of the destruction of war, but had been conscripted in the first year just as he was about to embark on a career as a professional pianist. On his first day at the battlefront in Egypt he was taken prisoner. After that life for him had been an unreal pattern of prison camps, hostels, huts, the journey to England, two years working on the land. Finally, after the war ended, settling down at the farm.

The two of them climbed over the middle gate and set off down one side of the home field. They were about the same height, but there the resemblance ended. Where Oliver was dark and thickly built, Mark was thin and fair. Where Oliver walked with the sturdy rhythmical gait of the natural countryman, Mark still walked with the stooping unco-ordinate movements of someone whose mind was very far from the green grass, the budding saps and the vagrant birds that were all around. Oliver was English and Mark was German.

This morning Oliver walked quickly. He was restless. Already his mind had turned back to the evening. He thought of Frances. What was it she had said? Sentimental. And then got annoyed. But why? Was that really what she had been annoyed about?

'We'll cut through the wood and take a look at the potato field,' he said gruffly.

About the farm Oliver saw everything as an item, the working material of the farmer's day. Even far out among the exposed fields his eyes were always examining the turf, the under-soil, the way the crops were lying. But the wood, which lay in the hollow between two of his fields, had become a romantic oasis in the matter-of-fact desert of his trade. He associated it with summer evening walks, Frances beside him, laughing at the chattering squirrels as they darted across the intermingled tree branches – with family picnics snatched between cleaning and the afternoon milking, Timothy and Theresa racing through the wood like wild Zulu warriors, howling bloodcurdling war-cries that echoed eerily among the trees. And there were strange, unrehearsed occasions when he came down on his own and strolled the length of the uncertain footpath and back again.

He never quite knew what made him come, nor could he satisfactorily identify the experience of his visit, but he always came away in some way refreshed, his mind clear, his body soothed. If he tried to analyse he was reminded of inadequate aphorisms; the quiet corners in every man's life, renewing from the secret pool, and so on. Some instinct always stopped him probing any further. He was content, surprisingly for one of his purposeful nature, to take no initiative in the matter, merely to accept with gratitude the familiar moods, the brief escape from his everyday self into some stranger that haunted the wood.

Today the wood was painted a gentle bright green by the sun, silvery shafts of sunlight piercing each chink in the leafy armour. Not for the first time he thought how it was like walking through a fairy country.

'In my part of Germany there are many woods, many

forests.' Mark was looking from side to side with quick appreciative nods. 'Some of them extend for hundreds of miles, even. But we have nothing that is quite like this.' He cupped his hands together and shaped them in a circular movement. 'How do you say it?'

'Pretty?'

'Yes. But something else. So small and yet so – full of everything.' Mark swept a hand round vaguely. 'Here there is everything that one could wish for, and all within arm's reach as you might say. In Germany one has to travel so far to reach everything one wants.'

'Yes, I suppose so,' said Oliver, not quite certain whether Mark was still talking only of woods. 'I always wanted to visit Germany. The Rhine, Black Forest, Heidelberg. I was friendly with a girl in London once, Ilsa her name was. She came from Wiesbaden. I remember her telling me how they used to spend holidays canoeing down the River Main. It sounded wonderful.'

Mark nodded.

'It is wonderful.' He shrugged. 'This, too, is wonderful. Life is full of many wonderful things. It is perhaps our own fault that we throw them away, or do not even grasp them when we have the opportunity.'

'Yes,' said Oliver. Noting Mark's slight frown, he wondered curiously what personal memories he was recalling behind the façade of the philosophic words. It struck him how very little he knew of Mark's world really, despite their frequent long discussions about the war and politics and the future and so on. Because he had a horror himself of divulging anything of his own privacy to the outside world, he was always extremely diffident about inquiring into other people's affairs. He had always found, anyway, that if people wished to talk about themselves they invariably did so without much prompting. Mark had never chosen to tell him anything more than that, before being called up, he lived with his mother and father and he had spent five years at a musical academy – oh, and yes he had mentioned that a gifted sister, who played the violin, had become a nurse. That was about all. He supposed that in effect he knew as much about Mark's life as Mark knew about his.

It was strange, he thought, the different worlds that existed, the world of men, and the world of women and men. There was for instance, no problem now between him and Mark, walking peacefully through the wood. But between him and Frances – between them there existed, he sensed, some most impenetrable problem. What?

'You've never been married, I suppose, Mark?'

He was surprised to hear himself speak. He hadn't meant to be so directly inquisitive. He looked quickly at Mark. He had expected to see the usual guarded look. Yet for a moment – was it his imagination? – for a moment, he thought he caught a flicker of brightness in Mark's eyes, as if unwittingly his words had pierced the armour.

'No,' said Mark evenly. 'I have never been married.'

Funny, Oliver thought. He could have sworn there was something. And it was disturbing. He felt almost as if he had said something he ought not to have said. As if in doing so he had unthinkingly set in motion a chain of words and thoughts, possibly actions, of which as yet he had no conception.

They came out of the woods and into the potato field.

'There's a branch there you can trim off,' he said automatically. 'I'll straighten this post.'

Now why had he spoken like that to Mark? Or rather, what was it he had really intended to say next? Why not go on talking peacefully about woods and rivers, remote girls one used to know? He had never before made any reference to Frances in front of Mark, or of anyone except Raymond. A man's marriage was his own affair, to make or mar as he please. His own marriage, he used often to think to himself, was a remarkably successful one. No one could have asked for a more wonderful wife. Frances was a constant source of strength and invigoration to him. It was on the sure foundation of herself and the children – he sometimes realised – that he had erected his whole life of progress and achievement. And there was no doubt but they made a handsome couple, he and Frances. The family made an attractive picture altogether: people were envious of their good fortune, of his in having such a lovely and alive wife, of hers in having such a successful husband, of them both in having two such delightful and intelligent children. God, it did sound a bit picture-bookish. He wondered if it ever struck Frances like that. But it wasn't their fault it was picture-bookish. It wasn't their fault their marriage had seemed peculiarly like a fairy-tale in its success and happiness – for after all, that was the point, it was a happy marriage.

At least, that was what he had always assumed. Perhaps taken for granted. He frowned, biting at his under lip, flicking with his stick at some rough weed. Odd that his mind should be spinning round and round like this, on a fair, untroubled morning. He shot a quick look at Mark, who was bending over the hedge, lopping off a tangled mass of briars. Odd, too, that he should have this feeling that Mark sensed the restlessness. Even, perhaps, that he guessed something of what lay behind.

Oh, but that was ridiculous. Their two lives were separate, belonged to different worlds.

But even as he thought thus, he was conscious of the same compulsion upon him to say more, to carry on from the single sentence he had left poised so uncertainly in mid-air.

'Do you not believe in marriage, then, Mark?'

He watched the other finish trimming the branch, then straighten up. He noticed that Mark looked across the field as he spoke, not at him.

'I believe in love. That is not always the same thing.' Mark's face softened and he smiled faintly. 'But do not think of me as a cynic. For obviously, if I say that it is not always the same thing, I imply that sometimes – possibly quite often – it is.' He ran his finger thoughtfully along the blade of the billhook. 'My mother and father were an example. They, I am convinced, were always deeply in love. It is a thing difficult to describe, but one knew it. It was in the atmosphere. My sister and I both felt it, we knew it was there. That was good, very good. But whether one is always so fortunate, well ...'

Oliver listened awkwardly. In the pause that followed he frowned, feeling that he was expected to say something, but unable to frame the words.

'No doubt you'll find out one day,' he said in the end, lamely, rather annoyed with himself. Or will you? he wondered. And how many do find out? he wondered. What is the end to the finding out? There is no end, he thought in some surprise, because one could never really be sure. And the gravity of this thought so impressed him that he hardly noted the ironic inflection in Mark's voice as he said, with a shrug:

'I hope I do.'

Suddenly Oliver felt his thoughts rising up to overwhelm him. It was as if there were a lot of dead stale thoughts that he had been fighting to keep in their place in his mind, about sacks of oats and calving and the new horse and the repair of the plough, and all at once they had tumbled out like unwanted rubbish. And in their place had rushed a heap of new thoughts that were strange and unfamiliar, and rather perturbing, mostly about Frances, and the haunting vision of her sitting up like a cold statue in the night.

He felt he wanted to be alone.

'Mark,' he said abruptly. 'Look, er –'

'Yes?'

He cast round in his mind for some purpose to give to Mark's departure. He supposed it was the subconscious part of his mind that made him say what he did.

'Look, I'd like you to go back now. I remember – my wife said something about sweeping out the yard. There's a lot of coal and wood logs ... the children have been throwing them about ... You go back, will you, and ask her what she wants done.'

It was as good a purpose as any, he supposed. And yet, even as Mark nodded and turned to walk back across the fields, he was conscious once again of some unwitting flaw in his own behaviour, of some unpredictable mistake which he had made for the second time.

He stood watching Mark's brown lanky figure as it moved steadily across the field, the fair hair blown awry in the breeze, and for a moment he was aware of an impetuous desire to call him back. If he had been a simple uninhibited native of the Stone Age tribes that were his natural forefathers he would possibly have obeyed the deep psychic impulses in him and cried out. But centuries of the neat ordered patterns of conventionality had completed their stranglehold too well, layer by layer, and he was powerless to act.

He stood there uneasily, his eyes straining until the brown speck had merged into the greater brown of the familiar earth, and then he turned and walked swiftly back towards the wood. As he went in under the great green awnings he felt weighed down with unfamiliar burdens, uneasily conscious that he was a traveller only on the beginning of a difficult journey.

'Can we play soldiers, Uncle Raymond?'

'Can we, Uncle Raymond?'

They were down by the reservoir. Here the sun poured lavishly upon the water, upon the grey parapets of stone and the long patch of white clay sand at one end where the water broke in tiny imitation waves. Over the other side of the parapet the land fell away sharply, as if this were some gigantic castle perched on top of the world – into the far distance you could see the wild Cornish moors basking in a sunny haze. It was ideal site for battles and assaults, for guerilla warfare, for scouting. And for invasion. Best of all they liked invasion, possibly because it gave Theresa, who was rather unenthused about other forms of warfare, an opportunity to play a suitably dramatic role.

'Let's play invasion!'

At the sound of the word Raymond groaned inwardly. He liked to help the kids have a good time. Already it seemed an eternity, twenty or even thirty years since his own childhood, yet in their company he felt some sort of a bridge across the ever widening gap. But hell, invasion. How lightly they talked about it.

Invasion. The gold-grey waters, the misty unfriendly outline of the land, the burst of smoke puffs, the grim squat shapes of pillboxes and iron fortifications – the warning rattle of machine-guns. Ahead the hypocritical smoothness of the sands, the Hampton Court maze of criss-crossing wirework and barbed stakes. Above them the twentieth-century vultures, fingers on bomb triggers, Death at a touch. Folly to go onward. Certain death. Stay back, stay back ... The memories poured over him in an avalanche. He gave a tiny cry and passed a hand across his head. Already, the familiar beads of sweat were forming, oozing into the cleft lines.

'All right, kids,' he said, with forced cheeriness. 'Invasion.'

Timothy clapped two approving hands.

'Come on, then.' His small but concise mind began framing the structure. Should it be a German invasion, in which case the defenders would gloriously triumph? Or a British invasion? – in which case the triumph would be reversed, of course. He decided on the latter since they had carried out a German invasion the last time. He issued his swift orders.

'Now then, Terra. You're a French peasant girl, see? You're the friend in the midst of the enemy. You've been waiting for this moment. You creep down to the beach and make signals to the waiting invaders. You'd better wave a handkerchief or something, like you're waving a flag. See? Hurry up. You go up the valley a bit then come down. And mind you don't let the Germans see you. You'd better crawl on your stomach.'

Theresa tossed her dark head, now neatly done up in a bun. Sometimes she wondered whether she ought to let herself be ordered about by a mere brother. But somehow she always found herself doing so. She rather liked it. She began walking back across the sands.

Timothy's mind hurried on.

'Now I'll go out on to the parapet and I'll be the British general.' He tightened his belt and adjusted his carelessly donned sweater.

'Uncle Raymond, could you – er –' He paused, struck by the fear that perhaps he was being rather insulting. 'Would you *mind* being the German general, defending? Would you? Just pretending you know ... You can be a field-marshal,' he added grandly.

Raymond laughed. 'Certainly, General Timothy. I shall be Field-Marshal von Raymondberg, heh?' He made a mock salute. Timothy, satisfied, ran off behind the parapet.

What was he supposed to do? Raymond laughed again, a

little hollowly. What did a German field-marshal do when faced
by an invasion? He knew damn well what they did when clearing
out a defeated British army. He began walking automatically
towards the sands, his mind darting back across the years. Yes,
he knew what they did at Abbeville. They bombed, and bombed,
and bombed. And he knew what they did at Dunkirk. They
bombed, and bombed, and bombed. And he knew what they
did at Benghazi, and Tobruk, and right up to the doors of Cairo.
They bombed, and bombed, and bombed. Until you became
just a piece of flesh rocking and quivering with the impact, not
knowing or caring what happened any more, just shaking like a
jellyfish until another jellyfish came and carried you away and
wrapped you up in blankets and put you in a throbbing van and
rattled you all the way back to the cool white sheets of some
Blighty hospital. And the bombs were still there, hovering
around, all the time you were in the hospital, and all the time
you were rocking gently in the homeward bound hospital ship,
right up into the port. The bombs followed you back to London
and East Ham and Barking Town. They followed you right out
of the Army into Civvy Street, were even with you when you went
down hop-picking in Kent.

There was no escape, no escape, no escape. No escape
anywhere, he thought wildly. From out of nowhere came a
familiar shrill whining scream, rising in volume. No, no, no ...
Help! He opened his mouth wide to scream. There was a faint
plop as the tiny sharp-edged pieces of stone fell harmlessly in the
water. He stood staring at the ripples stupidly, while his heart
thumped great irregular thumps.

'Hurrah! The British nearly scored a direct hit on the German
General Headquarters!' shouted Timothy, from behind the
parapet. Yelling wildly the British Commando Force came
pouring over the parapet, waving with magnificent grandeur a
wooden stick Bren gun. Before Raymond could, or dared, stir
himself, the commandos were all around him and past him.
There was a further hurrah as the invaders linked up with their
female friend against the enemy. A moment later the sharp
reprimanding point of a British Commander's baton stuck into
his ribs.

'Field-Marshal Karl Von Raymondberg, you are a prisoner of the British Army.'

Slowly, with an effort, he closed his mouth. He felt a few drops of revealing saliva slobber over his lips, and with a swift movement brushed them away. He counted the heartbeats; they were slowing, more regular. Give them a few moments more to settle down. Why did he have to give way so easily? Weren't the nightmares bad enough at night, alone in the labyrinth darkness of his room? Wasn't it bad enough to awake and find himself bathed in sweat, surrounded by the yellow, ghostly faces of the ones he had seen twist and crumple into the sands? Wasn't it bad enough to go through it all again, night after night, like some eternal routine? The guns increasing, doubling, trebling, quadrupling, multiplying into millions and millions of thunderclaps, all bursting upon him; the huge shadows of mountainous tanks, the fearful glint of blood-stained bayonets, a million of them diving straight at his guts. And then? Where did he go, where did he think he would go when he turned and ran and ran and ran and ran …? What did they think, as they lay draining their life's blood into the sands, mute and immobile?

Above all, what did Travers think, crouching low over his machine-gun, turning and watching him go with a wild, exaggerated look of incredulity disfiguring for all time his innocent face? He always came back to Travers. No one else knew. But Travers knew. Even if he was now sitting with God Almighty in Heaven, Travers knew. Knew the shame and the cravenness. Steady, steady now. The kids. Slowly, agonisedly, he forced a wide, insolent, sneering smile. He held up his arms.

'Field-Marshal Karl von Raymondberg at your disposal,' he said in an unfamiliar guttural voice. Turning, he allowed himself to be marched back, single file, to wherever German field-marshals were imprisoned.

And as he went the hot frustrated tears began to accumulate in his darkening eyes. It was a grim sort of joke when even the status of prisoner-of-war could only be attained by playing make-believe with children.

From the big bay windows of the kitchen, Frances saw the brown blob that was Mark come over the crest of the field and down towards the garden and the farmhouse. It reminded her of a dream, a recurring dream which had haunted her childhood, in which there was a figure approaching her from the horizon – only, in the dream, as the figure came nearer, so she felt herself receding, and it went on like that for a long time until suddenly she felt herself dropping right away, as if she had backed right out of the world into some dreadful void. When this happened she always awoke, sweating and trembling, convinced of the familiar hearsay of dreams, that if she had not awoken then she would never have awoken. But even that disturbed her less than the mystery of never knowing the figure, never seeing its shadowy face.

Now she wondered for a moment whether this was the dream, waiting in a strange daze to feel herself remorselessly pulled back and back ... Involuntarily she did step back a pace, banging into the table, rattling the mixing-cans and the heaped serving plates

'Are you all right, miss?' Edith, down on her knees and scrubbing a corner of the tiled floor, looked up inquiringly, blowing a fluff of red hair out of her eyes.

'All right?' Frances repeated the words mechanically, still staring out of the window, still clinging a little to the world of her dream.

Edith heaved her plump squat self upright and came over to the window.

'Oh,' she said, sniffing. 'Him. Looks as if he's coming this way, doesn't it? Mmmh.' She looked at Frances shrewdly. 'Mmmh,' she said again. 'Thought it was something exciting, bull got loose or a horse run away with your husband, maybe. It's not so long, you know, since Elliot, the man at Rawdon's farm, was charged by a pig and broke two ribs. Swore he'd never have anything more to do with pigs, either.'

She looked at Frances again, puzzledly.

'Ah, well ... It's only Mark, you know.' She resented situations which were too vague and intangible for her usual expert assessment. She shrugged. 'Ah, well, back to work.'

She got down laboriously, and rather noisily, upon her

knees, slopping the brush into the pail.

Mark was coming across the near field now, approaching the little wooden gate leading into the garden. He walked easily, sniffing the air; there was a look of unexpected youth about him. When he came to the little gate he vaulted over it and then came slowly across the garden, his blond hair puffing out in the breeze, looking with delight at the neat beds of flowers, the first buds colouring, here and there an early chrysanthemum, a bunch of hydrangea, like peeps of a rainbow.

The click of his iron-tipped boots on the cobbled yard struck across the haze of Frances' mind, shattering the mirror of her dream. So I am not asleep, she thought wonderingly. But then again – had she been asleep, was it the dream? Confused she raised a hand to her head and pressed the knuckles in. Then with a swift shake of the head she looked down at the basin, put her hands into the soapy water and began washing a glass dish.

Her head was bent, the gold-tinted hair falling forward like spray, when Mark appeared at the window, clearing his throat politely. When she looked up it seemed to him that the hair billowed out like gentle clouds, obliterating the room, the view, creating a sea-washed frame for the face. He had never seen her look so lovely. But he had never looked at her in quite the same way as now.

'Pardon.' He spoke softly. 'Mr Williams said I was to come to you.' He paused, whether on purpose or accidentally he could not be sure himself.

Frances stared blankly, her eyes wrinkled up.

'Oliver sent you? But –'

Mark smiled. In some secret way it was almost a teasing smile.

'Your husband said you might wish me to tidy the yard. He mentioned chopping some wood logs.'

'Oh yes.' Frances laughed, rather nervously. With a quick movement she pushed back her hair. In itself an innocent action, yet it seemed a decisive gesture, raising the curtain upon the remote enveloped world of two people looking at each other, opening the theatre, the side-galleries and the circles, to the large outer world. Through the exposed corner of the window Mark saw the rows of blue china plates, a kettle steaming on the stove, Edith's bent form, an inner life from which, he felt, Frances somehow remained apart.

He smiled again. This time it was unimportant, a politeness.

'Those are the logs over in the corner?'

'Yes.'

'You would like how many?'

It would not have occurred to him that these last words were in any way revelatory. But to Frances they were all at once a key, an illumination; they made him for the first time a reality and a person instead of a brown cypher. Deep down inside of her she could have wept at the tug at her heart when she heard the naïve, innocent words that were the flagpost of some entirely unknown, lost piece of humanity – but one that, she realised in all the fullness of the word, existed. The very preciseness of Mark's words became for her a puff of warmth, a part, almost like an arm or a leg, of some strange new character to which she had just been introduced.

'How many, please?'

'Twenty – twenty-five. Thank you very much.'

He nodded. The conversation was completed. He did not know whether it had been all that it should have been or not. That he would perhaps come to decide while he chopped the logs, in neat rhythmical movements.

He nodded again, smiled, and went across the yard to the pile of tree trunks and branches. As he picked up the chopper he felt her watching him through the window. He wondered how she was watching him; whether it was a peepshow on a poor German, whether it was part of some daydream of a woman at a sink, or whether it was as a face alone, guarded from watchers by cascading hair, confined again to the small private world between them. Because he did not know he dared not turn and look, but went on doggedly chopping and tearing at the odd shaped humps of wood.

And because she did not know either, Frances, too, did not look any longer but dropped her gaze back to the sink, and for the third time began methodically washing the glass dish.

Until there was another interruption, this time from elsewhere.

'Well, I don't know. What a row!' exclaimed Edith. 'Coming from the front.' She cocked a knowing ear. 'I thought so – that's the heavenly twins and Mr Raymond. What a row! I hope their feet are clean. I've just swept and dusted that hallway. It's too bad if their feet aren't clean.'

She disappeared into the interior of the house. Frances dried the dish, thoughtfully.

'Mum, mum, we've captured a real German field-marshal!' Timothy came bursting in with all the grandiose authority of one in his high military position.

Frances smiled, her heart swimming with tenderness for the tiny proud figure, the cheeky face looking up, the imitation wooden gun clutched tight between grimy fingers – and for the taller, almost ungainly figure of her daughter, who one day, she felt sure, would grow into a beautiful and sensitive woman. Much as she loved Timothy, his confidence and impudence, it was Theresa who captured her heart. In Theresa she saw all the raw material that had once been herself – in Theresa she was determined that it should be shaped to the most fruitful purpose.

'Sergeant!' Timothy called back, peremptorily, as a general should. 'Bring in the prisoner!'

Raymond came in slowly, his eyes still vague and shadowed from their thoughts.

'How do you do, Field-Marshal?' said Frances.

He did not look at her for a moment, but went and sank wearily into a chair, his elbows on the table, his head falling forward so that his dark unruly hair spread outwards like a shroud.

Frances stood for a moment; not surprised, for she was used to Raymond's burst of gloom and unhappiness, his utter dejection, his collapses; but in some way more perturbed than usual. How strangely silent everything could be. She could hear, in that poised moment, like the heavy ticking of a heart, the grandfather clock in the dining-room. Soon it would be time to make lunch. Another moment and back to the regular routine. Soon the clatter of footsteps, the patter of repetitive lunchtime conversations.

Then, her eyes falling, half unwillingly, on the stooping head at the table, she forgot her thoughts and instinctively stretched out a hand.

'Poor Raymond,' she said. A great pity came over her. She motioned the children to go into the hall, whispering to them that Aunty Edith needed their help.

She began, slowly and thoughtfully, running her fingers through his loose dark hair, starting at the top and feeling through to the soft flesh of his head. She drew his head to her side, a pillow for his weariness. Her hand wondered over his head and down his cheek and round his neck and back again. When they were close together, so much brother and sister, she was acutely receptive to his pain and suffering, even when she knew it belonged to a tortured inner world from which he could escape only by his own efforts.

'Poor Raymond. Poor Raymond.'

And then, almost without thinking, she looked out of the window and across the yard, and it seemed that just at that moment the man chopping the logs paused and half turned and stared. It was not that she met his eyes, or was even sure of the expression on his face, but she was aware that they were both looking for each other. She knew that even if he happened to see her standing there, stroking the huddled, unhappy figure of her brother, he would know, as she did, that she was comforting and whispering a sad hope for the whole unhappy world; that her love and sudden understanding was seeking out and reaching out to everywhere; and that in the very nature of things she was speaking to him when she whispered, Poor Raymond, poor Raymond.

The moment remained poised for a long time, with no movement and no happening. Then, like a strange but inevitable intruder, the clock in the next room began striking the hour. Frances took away her hand and walked over to the food cupboard.

'I must get on with lunch,' she said, in a cool, rather dry voice.

III

In the morning post, tucked between a bundle of bills and circulars from fertiliser manufacturers, was a letter for Frances. Purple-tinted envelope, sprawling handwriting in mauve ink – about it all an air of dishevelled hurry.

'Why, it's from Christine.'

She was genuinely surprised. It was seven years since she had last heard from this old, once very dear school friend. They had grown up together, adventured to London together, worked in the same publisher's office. Marriage had severed the knots; that and Christine's growing career in journalism.

'Goodness, she's been to America. As New York woman's correspondent for her paper. Fancy, she was there three years. Now she's back and working as a freelance. And – what's this? – Oh, yes, and writing another novel. Well ...' Frances looked guilty. 'I didn't even know she'd already written one.'

'What's her name?' inquired Raymond with professional interest. 'Her writing name, I mean.'

'Christine Adams.'

He shook his head.

'Means nothing. Perhaps she uses another name?'

'No, I remember she always vowed she'd never write under any name than her rightful one. She's probably terribly well known – just not your type of literature, darling. Of course, if she's got married or something ... But somehow I don't see Christine married.' She returned to the letter. 'Anyway, she doesn't say anything about it. Oh, how nice! She wants to know –'

She paused as Oliver came into the kitchen from the yard,

bringing with him the familiar smell of the cowshed, his gaiters caked with mud. He took them off and rubbed his boots carefully on the mat.

'Oh, Oliver, what do you think – a letter from Christine.'

'Not our one and only bridesmaid?' said Oliver ironically. 'I thought she'd long ago cut us off her list.'

'Don't be mean. She's been to America. And now she's back and wants to know if she can come out for the weekend. So there!'

'Well. Such loyalty.' He looked at her teasingly, loving the sudden animation that brightened her face, wishing he had inspired it.

Frances pouted, then smiled, already returning to the atmosphere of that past world which Christine's letter had suddenly revived.

'I wonder if she's changed much?'

'Probably,' said Raymond laconically. He remembered Christine vaguely. A smart, rather pretty woman, of whom he could recall hardly any more than that – and perhaps that her legs were nicely shaped. Odd to think of her as a fellow-writer, a colleague. He swallowed an angry exclamation. More than odd, humiliating – that 'writing another novel'. He thought morosely of his own heap of unfinished manuscripts, pages seared through with a savage miserable pen: the pile of short stories in which he could never quite believe, and which had brought, so inevitably, so many rejection slips. Nothing, not a single thing had he completed satisfactorily. But a slip of a blonde girl was writing her second novel.

'Shall we have her down, then?' said Frances eagerly.

'Why not?' Oliver's voice, at first sarcastic, softened, 'Of course, please do, Frances,' he said kindly. 'It will cheer you up. I know you've been feeling a bit depressed.' It was his first admission of anything untoward. He did not mean it to sound patronising.

'It will do us all good,' he went on. 'It will be someone new to argue with, won't it, Ray?'

'Certainly. Besides, I'm very curious to see how the fair Christine has progressed in her travels across the Atlantic and elsewhere. Write and tell her we're waiting with bated breath, Frances.' Raymond laughed. 'Oh, and by the way, as tactfully as you can, you'd better find out the title of her other novel – or possibly novels. From my own bitter experience I know only too well how galling it is for a writer to spend any period of time with people who have never read his work. Or her work, as in this case.

'Yes,' he said, swinging himself down from the corner of the table, 'it will be interesting to meet another writer. No doubt I'll be able to pick up one or two tips. How to be a Successful Writer.' Try as he would he could not keep the slight note of self-pity out of his voice. 'I only wish just one editor thought I was. Even a Promising writer with a capital P.'

Then, seeing from the uncomfortable silence that he was embarrassing them, he forced a chuckle.

'Oh, come, children, don't take me too seriously. As a matter of fact, the muse is at work in me now. I feel an irresistible desire for a typewriter and some paper. So excuse my sudden departure.'

He walked swiftly out of the kitchen, across the hall, up the big staircase. He was not one for facing the mirror; he averted his eyes until he had turned past it, went on with slow methodical steps. It was not true what he said with such sophistry, about the muse being at work. It was seldom if ever that he felt any natural desire for a typewriter and paper. It was always a battle with himself; it was only by a tremendous effort of the will that he forced himself to go up to that very lonely room, to sit at that excruciatingly bare desk, to pick up a sheet of that glaringly blank paper. When all that was done he began writing; at first with pain, but later perhaps with pleasure. It seemed a part of his destiny that so much had to be endured and fought for before he got any return, any satisfaction. He used to think that it must be the same for all writers; it probably was. But now he preferred not to think at all about other writers. Sometimes he thought that it was only by this pretence, even to the extent that there weren't other writers, that he found the courage to continue.

It had been different somehow when he was younger. Then

it was all new and challenging, like a glorious game. Then he had only to stare at a row of books, with the gold-printed titles and red-lettered author's names, and into his mind crowded streams of thoughts and daydreams. From the books his mind raced away to the worlds that lay beyond them – strange faces, coloured skins, tatooed sailors, big chattering dance halls, factories full of shrieking machines, furnace fires throwing shadows over a river – how he had longed to pin them down, to translate them into reality.

This part, the questing, the daydreaming, was not entirely gone. There were still times, as he sat tucked deep in the little attic in the remote house, when he stared at the blank sheet and his mind travelled across seas and continents … A Georgian wilderness or a Black Forest hut, a bridge in Austria with an old feather-hatted Tyrolean swinging his lantern by a mountain stream: oh, what were people thinking and doing at that moment in the yellow-painted tenements of Madrid? in the stony white kamooks of an Iceland waste? on the midnight aeroplane to San Francisco and the express train to Rome and the milk train to Adelaide? in the ten hundred coffee houses of Istanbul?

What were they saying, those couples and fours and sixteens, those families and thousands of families, sleeping and eating and dressing and talking and walking and grumbling and laughing and loving, all around – in the nearest house and the house after that, in the nearest street, and the street after that, in all the criss-crossing roads and villages and towns – in the ships moored down at the harbour, in some lonely aeroplane passing over – everywhere and anywhere, what was happening, what endless pattern of life was going on all the time?

He shook his head suddenly, finding himself on the top landing, standing with his hand on the doorknob. That was how it came and went. There would be moments like that; they came on him unexpectedly, perhaps when walking, perhaps when sleeping, perhaps when standing on a bridge looking into the river. Water fascinated, water that swirled towards him and then away. Just like those thoughts. That could never be captured. For when he went to the desk and attempted to paint them in the blue ink or the black typewriter ribbon, it was as if he stuttered and was at a loss for words. What he might manage to write down was never, he knew more truly than anything else in his life, that which had passed through his mind. It would be the pink shadow of the real red blood; the memory for the reality. Oh, he had tried. And tried and tried – until he screamed and threw the pen viciously across the room, screwing the sheets of paper into frenzied balls, scattering every item and object of his mesmerising possessions – ink, blotter, pencils, paper clips, once even the typewriter.

Before the war, he liked to think, there had always been hope, a prospect for some uncertain future. He had even thought the war might clarify, might time-bomb him into fulfilment. It was partly this conception that had given him the strength to go through with it, with all the months of deadly boredom intermingled with the horrifying bestiality of bayonet drill and other mild sports – things revolting to the core of his nature. But the war, for him, had been some private purgatory, just as now was the effort to go and write. It was the irreconcilable conflict that crackled like doom across the whole of his life: one part of him nagging him to go forward, trying to pretend that the achievement was possible, the other part of him giving way, like a rotting foundation, so that everything must always crumble and nothing be completed.

And that was how it had been in the war, he knew, when he was able to consider it soberly and objectively. He had tried to pretend there was not the fear whereas the fear had been the clay pedestal, the crumbling wall – in its weakness stronger than anything else. Perhaps if he had admitted that from the beginning, or even understood it, some solution could have been found. But he could never really admit it – not even now. Who could admit himself a coward? A failure? An unsuccessful writer? A washout, an anachronism? He had once read a philosopher's statement, intended to be consoling, 'the good lies at the bottom' – and laughed with venom. For he lived at the bottom, and in his secret heart he believed he had always lived at the bottom; and there was nothing to be found there in the way of hope or relief or comfort, only unbearable self-pity.

And so he had not even been able to put the war on to paper. You would have thought, even he had thought, that at least he could portray his own cowardice, his own emotional upheavals. But the truth was that when he tried, *every* time he tried, the waves receded, eluding his grasp, leaving him lost and crying for a dreamy past. And if he persisted those same waves mounted up into great white mountains and he knew they would come crashing down upon him with their own private nemesis; the vision of that French cornfield, the summer fruit trees like sentinels, the steel whipping tongue of the hidden machine-guns, the face of Travers in the unbelievably red corn ... Then he would scream and tear the sheet of paper into shreds. Into shreds, into shreds, into *shreds*!

And, looking down, he saw that his hands were trembling and there were frightened, crooked pieces of paper all around his desk, like snow that had fallen unexpectedly and would take some time to melt.

With a choked sob he sank down into his chair and buried his face in his arms – the furthest fingers touching, with expert frustration, the keys of the typewriter.

*

Frances came towards the little wooden hut in the early afternoon, on her way back from a walk through the woods. She had not any idea of calling there when she started, but she found herself thinking about Mark as she walked and the glimpse of the pointed wood roof egged on her curiosity. Ever since the morning that she had seen Mark's grave, rather quizzical face peering up at her through the kitchen window he seemed to have become crystallised in her mind. Now she was acutely aware of him as an individual and with this awareness came the intensification of her natural pity. She could not rid her mind of a sense of enormous guilt at the thought of this sad-faced young man being here, alone and unrecognised in an alien land, instead of – well, where?

She thought about that, as she walked down the fields, in the narrow space between the hedge and the first line of potatoes, and then climbed the stile into the cool wood. She tried to imagine the other world to which so much, indeed everything of Mark except his actual physical body, must belong. She tried to force her mind to travel hundreds of miles, across the great North Sea, over western plains, to some place, perhaps a village – but no, a town, she fancied; some tall, rather grim German industrial town – and she tried to conceive of people around him, a father, a mother, brothers, sisters, the clothes they wore, the lives they led, the life that he had led ... It was hopelessly unresolved, her mind only went round in a vast circle. Yet she kept returning and starting and going round in another circle, trying to put herself in his place, to feel as he would feel.

It was as she was reflecting how little she knew at all about his life that she came up over the mustard-and-cress field; the miniature gable-top of the hut caught her eye, and she was overwhelmed with a woman's fascination to peep into the unknown guardian shell of a man's life.

She knew he would be washing out the cow-shed preparatory to the afternoon milking, so she walked up to the hut quite boldly. It stood in a corner of the orchard, tucked under the shelter of two cherry trees with a hedge running behind, so that it seemed quite sheltered. Originally it had been a summer-house standing at the end of their front garden; some time later it had been moved away and used, she remembered uncomfortably, as a chicken-house. But evidently someone had given it a thorough cleaning and repainting. The outside walls were coated with bright green paint, the door was decorated with a crimson floral design. The two side-windows were still fresh with cream white paint, and the wooden steps leading to the tiny verandah were neat and carefully swept.

She pushed the door open and went in gingerly, smelling at once that curiously warming aroma of a man's room.

It was a room no larger than the children's bedroom, not much more than a box really. She was surprised at the ingenuity which had been expended on giving it a character and colour and warmth of its own. Down one side ran a narrow camp bed; she noted it had been tidied and covered with a green mat made from an old length of sacking. In one corner stood a small table and chair and in another a wash-stand made out of a packing case. In the centre of the opposite wall was a tiny brick fireplace, with the embers of a dead fire still scattered about.

A small unframed picture was pinned above the fireplace: a self-portrait. It was a clever likeness. The artist had caught some strange element of life, a glimpse of some secret vitality which she recognised now from having noted it in Mark's open smiling face.

She fancied the painting must have been done in Germany. There was a glimpse over Mark's shoulder of a window looking out on to a mountain, a scene she would not associate with Britain. And Mark was wearing what seemed like a ski-ing jacket. Whether he was really dressed for ski-ing she could not know because the picture ended at his waist. But the painter had shown Mark's hands – indeed, it was altogether unusual, as if Mark had been sitting with both hands raised in the air in front of him, poised and expectant. She wondered what it was that had so obviously possessed the entire concentration of the hands – what person, what object, lay forever tantalisingly outside the eye's scope.

They were long thin hands, almost like sculptures, yet even in the picture there was a hidden strength about them. She noted the protruding gauntness of the wrist bones, the fan-like patterns of the fingers, the skin taut and veiling a hundred streams of red and blue veins that wandered across the back of each hand like some malignant growth. The veins were lost in the clean whiteness of the fingers, fingers which stretched out long, unbelievably long – like an eagle's talons. So white were the fingers that they might have been nothing but glistening outlines of polished bones.

Frances stood close to the picture and stared fascinatedly at the fingers. It looked as if the finger nails had been cut unnaturally short, flesh grown up around them so the tips were rounder and more fleshy than any other part of the hands. They were round and fleshy finger-tips, worn into grooves. Suddenly she realised that the artist had devoted an enormous, minute attention to the two hands – more than to any other part of the portrait. The hands held a peculiar significance. Indeed, in some way, they were a key to the whole picture, to the whole character.

She could not take her eyes off the small rectangular picture, now faded from the passage of years, stained in one corner by drops of coffee. She was still staring at it when, softly, the door swung open and she was aware of his presence close behind her.

'Oh!' She turned round nervously, lowering her eyes. 'I – I don't know what to say. Please forgive me. I am not in the habit of prying like this into people's privacy. I –'

'Please.' He was smiling. 'It is no matter. Privacy, as you call it, has been absent from my life for quite many years.' He raised a hand to cut short her further protest.

'Please, you are very welcome. I do not often have visitors.'

The quiet irony struck her to the heart. She looked away.

'I don't think I have quite understood before now – well, the loneliness. After all this time. I do hope – perhaps it won't be long now before you go back.'

She had to force out the superficiality, and even the echo sounded hollow. Then he motioned to the chair.

'I think I ought to be getting back.' Frances hesitated, aware of Mark's steady gaze. She felt herself blushing slightly and was annoyed. 'I feel most embarrassed, coming into your room like this. I mean, I would be most annoyed to find you in my room. Why should I be in yours? It was only that, I wondered – well, if you were reasonably comfortable and – and –'

Her face looked so downcast that Mark burst out laughing.

'It is not important. Really.'

Frances found herself laughing, too.

'Well, thank you for your forgiveness. I really must go.' She looked again at the portrait. 'I was admiring your painting. Is it by yourself?'

'No. It was done for me by a friend. A very gifted boy who was with me at the university.'

'It's very well done. Was he going to be a professional painter?'

'He was – unfortunately a British sniper blew his brains out at Benghazi.'

Frances was silent. Now it was his turn to look uncomfortable.

'Please. I do not mean to be rude. These things were all madness. Let us hope they are finished with.'

He looked quizzically around the room. Following his gaze from one to another of the few desolate objects, Frances felt pity sweep over her at the thought that what he was looking at was all, everything, that there now was in his life.

But no, not everything, surely.

'Do you hear often from home?' she asked gently.

He raised his eyebrows.

'There is no one to write.'

She was horrified.

'But surely – I mean – what about your parents?'

'My father and mother and my younger brother were killed in an air raid. Our house was wrecked. I only heard this a long time afterwards, through another prisoner.'

He did not know what made him tell her. Some inner bitterness had prevented him from mentioning it to a soul in all the time since he had heard; for three years it had nestled and festered, one of many sores that had never ceased to blister deep down within him. Now, merely to expose it gave him a sense of relief.

'But – but –' The enormity, the insurmountability of his loss fell upon Frances like a great weight.

It was he that smiled. She wondered how he could ever smile again.

'Do not be sad, not now. Once I was sad to the point of madness. But I came to learn – nothing in life is unendurable. That is one of many things I have learnt during my period of enforced exile. One can only accept – everything – and go on. One should be glad of the happiness that there was.

'That is how I think about my parents – there was much happiness and now it is finished. But there are other things. There is still one person – a sister. She was not at home at the time. She may still be alive – one does not know. It is sad. I have been unable to get in touch with her. She seems to have disappeared. But one day I shall find her.'

Frances walked over to the window. He wondered if she was going to cry. If she did, he felt he would be annoyed. He could endure anything, but not the English sentimentality.

'No, I am not crying,' she said, divining his thoughts (how and why she should do so was something likely to trouble her greatly).

He looked at her thoughtfully his eyes tracing the colourful floral pattern of the cotton dress, the neat, finely shaped line of her back and the swell of her hips. He was aware, not for the first time, of a surging warmth towards her; stranger, Englishwoman.

'I won't cry,' she repeated. 'But I'm appalled to hear it all. What must you feel? How could you bear – Oh, I'm sorry, I don't mean to pry.'

'It is very nice,' he said shortly, 'that someone should want to pry.'

'You have borne your sorrow well. But you only pretend when you say you are not bitter, don't you?'

For a moment, for the first time, he let fall his massive defences.

'Bitter? Oh, yes. I am underneath considerably bitter. I am so because I was on the threshold of a life, and now I must remain forever on that threshold, that life can now never be. Do you wonder I am bitter?'

But he spoke in generalities. As yet he couldn't bring himself to expose his real, terrible frustration, he could bear not to think of it let alone speak. Then his eyes came to rest on his hands, held out in front of him, fanwise. And as he looked at them they began to tremble, as if fearful of their revelation.

Frances followed his gaze, saw the hands, and was filled with a strange curiosity; yet something stopped her from asking.

After a moment he brought his hands down to his side and carefully clenched his fists, as if to banish the feelings that had swept over him.

Frances moved towards the door, restlessly, still conscious of some part of the room that eluded her grasp. She hesitated with her hand on the knob.

'Are you happy here? I mean is there anything – ?'

He pondered gravely.

'I think I am less unhappy here than anywhere else I have been in this country. Your husband is a good employer. I think we understand one another.'

'I'm glad. Most people seem to agree on that.'

'I think it makes a great difference that your husband is not a bully or a slave-driver.' Mark smiled faintly. 'You have no idea how important that is. Some of the farmers I have worked for – well, I think they thought we were back in the slave age, or otherwise the Germans were some sort of extra-animals. At least that was how they treated us. But your husband is not like that.'

'And here – this hut – it is comfortable?' she asked doubtfully.

Mark smiled.

'It may seem strange to you, but I value being alone, having this small room of my own. You may say that I have had enough loneliness in the past few years. But that has been more the loneliness of separation from those one knows and loves. Physically I have been surrounded on all sides, inescapably, by people. So I am only too glad to escape now, to have this – how would you say – retreat?'

He waved his hand round.

'Books help – I like reading, it soothes.'

Frances looked at the small heap of books, with the gold and black Gothic printing. They were pitifully few.

'In that case – we have quite a large library.'

'Yes, I have looked at it once or twice, through the window. It was good to see.'

'But please let us lend you a few books. They would be English, I'm afraid.'

Mark's face lit up.

'But yes, that would be a great favour.'

'Are there any books you particularly want? We have quite a choice.'

'I am sure.' He bowed. 'I leave the choice to you.'

'Oh, but I might choose something you'd hate. No, obviously, the best thing will be for you to come and choose for yourself.'

'That I would like ... so long as it is agreeable to all.'

'But of course, I'm sure Oliver will be only too glad.'

'As long as it is agreeable to all,' repeated Mark doggedly.

Frances stared for a moment.

'You mean Raymond? But he won't mind –'

She stopped, knowing deep down that, for some strange reason, Raymond might take offence. She shrugged. Oh, well, she would see to that. She was impressed, nevertheless, at Mark's intuition.

'I do not think that your brother likes me very much.'

'I shouldn't bother about that too much. Raymond is – well, a little highly-strung.'

Mark hesitated.

'He is very highly-strung. And very unhappy. That is not a good state to be in.'

'Oh, well ...' Frances smiled. 'You have full permission to go to the library any time you wish to take out a book.'

'It is good of you. I will of course come to your back door first, in any case.'

Frances looked at her watch.

'Goodness, I must go.'

Mark bent down and opened a drawer, rummaged and brought out a handkerchief.

'If I may – I will walk back with you. I must attend to the milking. I just slipped back for this.'

'Very well.'

Frances went out into the sunshine. There was a faint breeze that ran in and out of the grass like a lazy fish in some placid sea. She watched the blades furrowing this way and that. She was conscious of a restive sense of peace. Looking out over the long rolling fields, and the neat red-tipped lines of the farm buildings, she felt a contentment that she could not explain.

Mark came out, his eyes blinking in the bright sunshine. He had taken his brown coat off and carried it over his shoulder. His arms hung at his side, his hands relaxed and forgotten.

They began walking back across the field, both looking ahead, both occupied with the wandering thoughts of a sunny afternoon. But before long, almost without noticing the change, they were talking animatedly.

*

On the Saturday evening Oliver drove Frances in the Lagonda to Bedruthan to meet Christine. As the London train was not due in until nine o'clock they were going to have dinner first at the Antelope Hotel. Frances had put on her new green dress, Oliver had changed from his muddy farm clothes into a brown tweed jacket and grey flannels. It was an outing they frequently made, a pleasant break snatched from the unending routine of farm life. Sometimes they went on afterwards to the pictures, or called in at the local Young Farmers' Club, of which Oliver was chairman. There was always a tinge of excitement, an exhilaration, about this going out alone together, even after all the years. It was a precious time that they both valued greatly, without ever saying as much. They awaited it eagerly, and they always came to it in good humour, and throwing away the cares of the week.

And yet it was not quite the same this time, Oliver decided, swinging the big green roadster between the farmyard gates and down the grassy lane to the main road. He was conscious in some subtle way of Frances' presence beside him being withdrawn, so that a greater distance than the inches of space existed between them.

The sense of separation grew, irritating him because of his desire for talk and companionship. As often when upset or peeved he found a solace in driving, coaxing the Lagonda into higher and higher speed, becoming frozen into a part of the car itself, so that he felt himself moving and acting as another unit in the taut machinery.

Once they were on the main road he pressed his foot hard on the accelerator, listening to the slow rising whine of the super-charged engine as it rose, almost protestingly, to a full throttled shriek. He knew the four miles stretch of road into

Bedruthan blindfolded. It was for the most part a long straight stretch, with a few gentle curves that could safely be taken – or at least which he would take – at sixty-five miles an hour or even more. He crouched down lower into his seat, bending his face forward slightly so that his eyes were watching in two pin-point lines just above the top rim of the light mahogany wheel; his gloved hands resting lightly on either side of the wheel, one finger caressing the cross-bars gently. Everything else faded and was lost from him: there was only this thing, the whining noise shrieking him along the lonely grey road, like a meteor bound for the distant lights.

Above all, he liked driving at night. Then, he sometimes felt, the car became something without any relation to outside circumstances, a tiny dark silent globe that was spinning its own purposeful way across whole continents, lands and seas and mountains. At night he was a private god and this was his kingdom, this long sleek green shape with the big red leather plush seats, with the scratched mica windows, the windscreen still marked with old bloodstains of a stray bird that had not been quick enough to avoid its hurtling doom.

Often in the evenings he would take out the car merely for the sake of driving, revving up the big twelve-cylinder engine and booming away into the darkness, his eyes absorbed in the fleeting pattern of worlds that were momentarily captured and frozen in the silver-white arc of the headlamps; rainy pools winking silver, a lonely signpost, the gaunt waterworks building, the dark sleeping roofs of cottages, sometimes a lovering couple wandering down the lanes – all pin-pointed and exhibited mercilessly, then gone, gone forever, never to be again.

When he was held in the grip of this triumphal aloofness he would drive for miles and miles, foot hard on the accelerator, swinging round corners, changing down only for the hair-pin bends, then declutching and roaring away into the straight infinite distance ahead. He was a god and his world went with him: the only requisite was speed, speed, speed, the sense of flying through the air faster and faster, perhaps faster than anyone else, faster than sound, on and on and on ... Speed fascinated him because of its quality of infinity, because it sometimes seemed to him the one thing in life which had no end to it, and therefore the greatest challenge of all.

Before the war he had driven the Lagonda in one or two road races. The experience had been exhilarating, almost irresponsible, in its abandoned ecstasy. He longed again to experience the thrill of competition, of becoming super-human, manhandling the car round corners and into skids out of which you wouldn't normally have expected anybody to emerge. He supposed there was some revelation of his character in this secret passion. He could imagine what people such as Raymond – the intellectuals – would have thought of it: a childish game.

Yet, he thought resentfully, why was it any more childish than rock-climbing or chess or just talking, all intellectual pastimes? Did they but know it, speeding in a motor car contained in its mysterious secretive centre just as many elements of aesthetic experience, of spirituality, as anything else. Of that he was convinced during those strange, sometimes disturbing nights when he crouched alone, free from the contacts and claims of the human world, feeling the whole shimmery shape of the car trembling, watching in detached surprise the white and green and gold shadows of the outside world streaming towards him and then into the void; hurtling from nowhere into nowhere, beyond knowing or caring whether the car held the road or whether it roared off into the very sky.

But tonight he was not alone. He was well aware of that. It was as some gesture – a defiance, a punishment, he was not sure which – that he kept his foot down hard on the accelerator, even as they approached the first bend leading between the houses of Bedruthan.

'Oliver! Please – don't be mad. Slow down or you'll kill us!'

Her voice trembled, partly with anger, also underneath with fear. He was satisfied. Perhaps it was schoolboyish, yet he had forced her to emerge from her privacy; now he relaxed, was ready to be human, friendly.

'Sorry.' He grinned sheepishly. 'You know what I get like,

driving at night. You should be used to it by now.'

'Well, I think it's stupid.'

She spoke crossly, aware that her heart was still beating with nervous flutters. She knew he had done it merely to impose himself on her in some way or other. That was why she had sat there for so long, clenching her teeth, determined not to cry out. But that last moment, she really had thought they would topple over. He was a reckless idiot. She could almost hit him.

Yet when he grinned at her like that, she found it hard to remain cross.

'It's a wonder we didn't arrive here in an ambulance,' she said primly as they drew up outside the hotel. 'Another time I'll drive.'

Oliver laughed with heavy sarcasm. He got out and went round to open the door.

'Here we are, madame. Dinner is waiting.'

He helped her out, then locked the car up while she straightened her clothes and patted back her hair, with its twinkling gold spangle. They went in through the pillared entrance; a tall, smart, rather attractive couple.

By the time soup had been served and the waiter had brought a bottle of Chianti, she had thawed. He was once more bubbling with good humour, joking about Christine, about the children, about Mark.

As he mentioned the name her eyes flickered. In the car when they started out she had been thinking about Mark; why she did not know or trouble to reason, but it seemed that she could not get him out of her mind, as if she must always be trying to piece together the fragmentary, pitiful shape of his life. She burned with an inexplicable urge to know his life, its core as well as its fringes. The speeding in the car had driven the thoughts away. For a time she had been thinking of, talking only to, Oliver. Now he himself brought the reminder. It was almost as if she were meant to unravel the secrets, one by one, as if she must not stray from that.

'Oh, I was talking to him today,' she said casually. 'Mark, I mean. Somehow I hadn't realised before – how horrible it must be for him – alone.'

'I don't think it worries him as much as it might some of them. He's a pretty self-possessed fellow, you know,' said Oliver, remembering the baffling smile. 'He doesn't let much out either.'

Frances hesitated.

'He told me that his people were killed in an air aid. He has no one – only a sister who *might* be alive.'

'Good Lord!' Oliver stared. 'Why, he never so much as hinted at that. You must have thawed him out quite a bit. What else did he say?'

'Oh, nothing much. I – I said he could borrow books from our library.'

'Good idea.'

Frances frowned.

'Funny – he seemed to think Raymond might object.'

Oliver took a sip at his wine.

'So he might. You know the bee in his bonnet about running away from Germans. But I'll explain to him, somehow.'

He stretched a hand out and rested his fingers lightly on Frances' arm. 'Nice of you to bother, darling. I quite agree. I often feel uncomfortable to think of the poor fellow out in that hut. But – he seemed keen to be there.'

'Oh yes,' said Frances quickly. 'He likes to be alone, to think and read.' She blushed gently, feeling Oliver's gaze suddenly shift from the wine to her.

'By the way,' she said quickly. 'What was Mark – I mean, what did he do before the war?'

Oliver shook his head.

'Search me. We shall only know if he chooses to tell us.'

He sipped at his wine again. His eyes were looking across the dining-table, to the long sideboard, the neat stacks of cutlery, the rows of plates; the cruet, glasses, a flower pot. Order and familiarity – sometimes he felt strange rustlings of wind on the horizon, a foreknowledge of disruption to come. He shook himself irritably. When he turned and looked back at Frances his eyes were shadowy.

'Enjoying it?' he said.

Frances smiled.

'Yes, lovely. And you?'

'Oh, yes. Yes, fine.'

They ate on in silence, he the steaming goulash and the red carrots and roast potatoes, she the delicate white plaice and the parsley and finger chips. It was a tasty, well-cooked meal, as nice as any before; the room was busy with the hum of conversation and the brightness of different faces; they were yet another smart couple, enjoying an outing. But things were not quite as they were. Nothing was neat and tied up; far beneath there were uneasy currents that tugged this way and that, the more disturbing because they were never quite recognised by either of them.

'Oliver, I can't bear this – this void,' said Frances desperately. 'Quick, let's drink a toast.' She held up her glass bravely. 'Here's to you and me.'

'OK. To you and me.' Oliver grinned. 'And the rest. To Tim and Terry and Raymond, to the farm and everything else that belongs to our lives. Eh?'

'Uh-huh.' Frances nodded.

The glasses clicked. They drank. The wine was cool and clear. It coursed through them with a sweet warmth.

But when it was drunk, it was drunk. And there remained about them the atmosphere, hanging heavily like clouds of troubles.

Oliver sighed. On the way back, he reflected, he would see if they could touch eighty on the stretch of Billington Woods. Damn and blast, he thought, itching to get his thick rough hands on the polished steering wheel, to plunge into the escape of the darkness and the godhead arc lights.

'Come on, then,' he said, pushing back his chair. 'Let's meet that train.'

IV

They had their Sunday picnic along the edge of the reservoir, sitting on rugs spread out over the sloping green bank. It was like being at the seaside. An afternoon breeze ruffled the great sheet of water, puffing up tiny waves that raced along and shattered themselves against the stone parapets. A rickety platform on thick wooden stilts ran out towards the centre of the reservoir, just like a pier. There was even a boat, a white dinghy, bobbing up and down near the end of the platform, a solitary fisherman squatting on one corner with his long rod reaching up, silhouetted against the horizon. Close your eyes slightly, as Timothy and Theresa might do, and you could imagine it was the seaside on an early summer day; you could imagine Channel mailboats, the *Queen Elizabeth*, the old *Mauretania*, France and the Breton fishing smacks lay just over the horizon. Perhaps it really was the sea but required the innocence and imagination of a child to perceive it. For the jaded adult eye the horizon was a long row of straight poplar trees, an iron bridge, hedges, the distant outline of farmhouses and the Penwith hills rising like some strange other country.

'Isn't it heavenly?' murmured Frances.

She lay back, pillowing her head against her folded hands, watching a few late clouds scurrying across the blue afternoon sky. Faintly she could hear the excited shouts of Timothy and Terra, scrambling over broken parts of the parapet to reach the grey sandy edge where the water ended. She smiled as she heard Timothy shrieking, 'Uncle Raymond! Jump now, Uncle Raymond, or the guards will get you' – her body faintly aglow with the pleasure of their pleasure.

She felt rather guilty to think of how long it was since she had come down with them. She mustn't let them grow disappointed, turning to Raymond as a replacement. It wasn't that she neglected them, but somehow these last few days she had found it difficult to concentrate her thoughts on them, or on anything in particular. She wished she could, wished it were possible to marshal the elusive floating fragments into some semblance of coherence. Right now, though, she must concentrate on being a good hostess.

She sat up abruptly.

'Christine. Another cup of tea? I think there's some left in the thermos. And please do help yourself to the sandwiches. It's home-made cheese.'

She smiled affectionately as the girl in the powder-blue dress nibbled with extravagantly displayed pleasure at the sandwich. How odd, and yet how nice – how much the same as it had always been – to be sitting here beside Christine. She had changed very little: or perhaps they, their relationship, had changed little. Of course, Christine was more mature, sometimes alarmingly sophisticated. Now and then she made Frances feel something of the country cousin. But she remained the old, sweet humorous Christine, with whom she used to write scurrilous poetry about the headmistress.

Frances giggled.

'I wonder what's happened to Clarky?'

'Why, I'm sure she's still there, rearing the young English gentlewoman of tomorrow. Dear Clarky!' Christine sighed. 'I wonder if she ever wonders what's happened to us?'

She sat up and looked around, patting her hair straight. She was not really pretty, but had what men would call an interesting face. It was more striking in profile: the curved nose, the firm mouth, the set of the chin, all indicated a very determined young woman.

'You know, Frances, I often used to try and imagine where you lived – the farm, the background, the children. The funny thing is, it was almost exactly like this. I hope you don't mind my saying so?'

'Of course not.'

'I mean, if I was trying to be catty I could be hinting that you'd done something humdrum and conventional. I don't mean that at all. What I mean is …'

Christine hesitated, looking at Oliver lying on the ground, staring into the lapping water.

'Well, wherever I've been in the last year or two, there's been such a restlessness, people running here and there. Here there seems such a sense of peace. You've no idea what a relief it is.'

'Peace is relative,' grunted Oliver without looking up.

'Cynic,' laughed Christine. 'I've a good mind not to pay the compliment I was going to.'

Oliver swung round and sat cross-legged.

'Oh, come, please do. We're always avid for compliments, aren't we, Frances?'

'Too true.'

'Well, I was only going to say that I think you two ought to be proud about this peace. I don't just mean the place, the country and so on – it's something else, something you've created yourselves. It's all bound up with you two, and Timothy and Theresa there, and building up the farm – a life you've made.'

Christine took a large bite at her sandwich. She had pretty teeth, thought Oliver. He liked her. She was a type, frank and open, that he understood and admired. All the same, seeing her only emphasised to him how glad he was that he had married Frances, someone who had miraculously escaped the standardising polish of the sophisticated world.

'Now I suppose you'll be putting us in your next book?' he said teasingly.

Christine regarded him contemplatively.

'That's not at all a bad idea, Oliver. Perhaps I will.'

And suddenly he felt annoyance sweep over him, almost a petulance, found himself resenting the very fact that there could be even joking references to his and Frances' life. Why should it be exposed like this, held up for examination – why, oh why, could it not remain safely tucked away and inviolate? Why must the curtains lift, the sudden unwelcome draughts of cold air blow in? – he knew, bitterly, that no matter what he wished, that was what had happened.

So he did not answer Christine but turned back to the water, to watching the criss-crossing waves weaving their endless and yet unreal pattern, that could be seen but never grasped.

Christine frowned inquiringly at Frances, but Frances had turned away quickly to avoid just such a look.

'Here's Mark coming along the path,' she exclaimed, glad of the respite. 'I wonder what he wants.'

Oliver stirred unwillingly.

'I told him to call me when the cows were ready.'

'This is that German ex-prisoner I was telling you about,' Frances said to Christine. 'The one whose people have all been killed.'

'Poor devil,' said Christine. She turned and watched the tall, blond-tipped figure coming along the path. Oliver watched too. Frances wondered if Mark was conscious of their concentrated stare. It was almost as if he was a character in a play, one with apparently the smallest of parts: his merely the duty of making an entrance, announcing that the cows were ready and then departing – and yet somehow she felt an implication that the part was really far more important.

Whether or not he was aware of their watching, Mark continued to walk in the same unhurried fashion, swinging his arms loosely.

'Curious what long arms he has,' commented Christine. 'Have you noticed?'

'It's funny you should say that,' began Frances. 'There is something strange about his – well, his hands.'

'Strange how?' queried Oliver, still watching.

Frances blushed.

'Oh, I don't know. Just an impression I got. I really don't know.'

Raymond's dark head appeared beside them, as he climbed up from the sands. He was flushed from his exertions in chasing Timothy and Theresa.

'Hullo, how goes it? I think I've fobbed the little vagrants off for a while. Any sandwiches left?'

Hungrily he picked up the packet and began eating. He

looked from Oliver to Frances puzzledly, then followed the line of their gaze.

'Oh.' He paused with the sandwich half-way to his mouth. 'What does he want?'

His tone was suddenly hard.

'Why isn't he working?' he went on savagely. 'You shouldn't allow this slacking, Oliver.'

'Don't be childish,' said Oliver wearily. 'I asked Mark to call me for the milking.'

He got to his feet as Mark came up.

'All right, Mark, I'm ready.'

Mark nodded and smiled at Frances. How strange, she thought, even his one speech isn't necessary; and again she was convinced it was all part of a play. And when her thoughts were over and gone, she found that she was smiling back at Mark.

'Good afternoon,' she said suddenly. 'Mark, this is a friend of ours, Miss Adams.'

It was some additional dialogue, unnecessary perhaps; she did not know. Mark bowed and smiled. Christine nodded. Raymond looked away sullenly. How silly, how childish, Frances thought angrily. The war's been over years. He's no longer a prisoner, he's an equal, a fellow human being. But still hundreds of miles from his home – that is, the home he used to have. She felt a sudden desire to grasp Raymond by the shoulders, to pull him round, to force him to smile at Mark. Oh, but it was stupid to get excited. Raymond was entitled to his opinion. She sighed, weary at the prospect of battling with Raymond's stubbornness. As stubborn as Oliver, in his own way. It was a relief to have Christine here, another woman, not always to be fighting stubborn wills.

She looked up at Mark quietly, as he stood back waiting for Oliver to put on his coat – was he, too, stubborn? She found herself observing the lines of his face, the strong nose, the thick, curling lips, the polished cheekbones, the ... Then he turned and eyed her fully, and she felt a shock as their eyes met, at the look he gave her – a look containing a solid strength of purpose that shattered all her scaffolding of cobwebbed excuses. For, at last, it dawned on her that to say that she felt sorry for him would be to leave something unsaid.

'Come on,' said Oliver tersely. Without looking, he had sensed the moment, the look. 'We've work to do.'

They trudged silently back along the towpath, each absorbed in his thoughts, neither seeing the wild waving of Timothy and Theresa, nor hearing the excited sandboy cries as they scavenged for strange fish and coloured stones.

Frances watched them go in silence, the two tall figures that walked in unison yet were so different, fashioned out of stranger-worlds; two such separate creations that were yet, deep down, both men; as wilful, romantic, unpredictable, illogical as all men.

'They seem to get on well enough,' commented Christine.

'Too well,' said Raymond shortly. 'There's no need for Oliver to be quite so effusively pally.'

'Oh, Raymond! Really!' cried Frances. 'How can a man of your sensitivity have such a blindspot? Oh, I'm sorry, I know it's hard for you. But there's no need to be so rude about Mark.'

'I know ... I know.' His tone was familiar to Frances, flecked with the deep-rooted, irremovable bitterness. 'I know I'm being irrational – you know that.'

He was looking at her now, directly at her, as so often; pleading, demanding something of her, some sign of comfort. But she could not, she could not always be his refuge.

'After all, the war already seems a bit dim, doesn't it?' said Christine mildly.

'Dim?' echoed Raymond. 'Dim?'

And the word seemed indeed like an echo that had slipped into his head and was now spinning backwards and forwards on an interminable journey, buffeted here and tumbling there, booming and reverberating through the dark corridors of the castle that was him; dancing in ghostly waltzes in the hallways and the chambers, the banqueting rooms and the cellars, ever gathering nearer to the tiny secret room where the castle jewellery was contained – where, in their last refuge, his brains stood on a marble plate like strange exhibits waiting to be pounced upon, waiting for the inevitable stroke that would split them asunder, that would hurtle them from their ordinary pedestal into their long foreshadowed chaos.

'Dim?' said Raymond, and now he had risen slowly, though he did not know it, and was standing half turned towards the reservoir so that to him it seemed, as to children, like a sea – but to him it was a sea that always lay between him and the desired shores; he was always alone in some solitary dark place, and there was always a wide sea, and beyond it lay all the things in his life that he wanted, or thought he wanted. They were there, vague shapes on the horizon, swaying gently in the breeze; but before him was the wide silver sheet, the white-kissed sea, the water that hated him, the water that was the blood of a million men down the million centuries, blood and water, water and blood, oh blood, oh blood ... blood of all our times. And dim – it was dim, she said, already it was dim?

He stared at Christine, his mouth sagging with incredulity.

'How can you say that?'

She looked uneasy.

'Christine didn't mean to sound flippant,' said Frances soothingly. 'She was only trying to emphasise that the war *is* over, that the fighting and the killing is finished, thank goodness. That it's done with now, forever we hope. Surely you agree?'

'Agree?' said Raymond dully. 'Who am I to agree?' His eyes focused again, now burning with their inner emotions. He clasped his hands behind his back and began pacing up and down.

'Christine, I'm afraid you will think me a little odd, a little – crazy perhaps. I can't help it. I am not –' He paused. 'I am not – what I was. I wish perhaps I had known you when I was a little boy. When Frances and I were little ... oh, the fun we used to have, the wonderful dream worlds we built and lived through and built anew. Didn't we, Frances?'

'Yes, dear.'

Raymond looked across at Timothy patting into shape a child's castle, at Theresa binding grass stems together.

'Just like them, now. But it seems a hundred years. And in that hundred years I have changed. Other people may have changed, too, I know nothing about that. I am no other man's keeper. I am my own – and the task fills me with terror. For there is no world left for me which I am fit to inhabit. Do you understand? There is no peace, no calm, no place of rest. Can you comprehend that? Of course you can't. Or perhaps in a way you can. I thought perhaps so, when you were talking about peace ...

'For some people there is never peace, there never can be peace. Can you imagine how they feel, those who know that? – who know that however long the life stretching ahead of them they can never, never rest?'

'I think many of us experience that feeling at some time or other,' said Christine evenly. 'It is a private battle we each have. It is up to us whether it is – concluded. Or whether it goes on until we are exhausted and give up. Which, I imagine, is hellish.'

Raymond nodded his head slowly.

'Which you imagine is hellish. Oh yes, it is hellish. But you talk of battles – what do you know of battles?' In his voice there was a strange but impersonal scorn. 'All our airy philosophers and novelists, our preachers and painters, always spouting about battles of the soul, conflicts of the mind – they are talking in theories. Theories, do you understand? What do they know of the *reality* of battles? What do they know of physical stabbing, shooting, bloody killing? That is the only real battle, the battle of men spilling their own blood. And you know as well as I do that the only people who can endure it are the ordinary dull-witted, the convention-blinded, the suburban average everyday unimaginative man – the dull stupid peasant to whom it is all part of daily existence. They it is who leap over trenches and capture uncapturable machine-gun posts, who dive under tanks, who bayonet the other fellow to butchered pieces ...'

Raymond's breath hissed out.

'But what about the *imaginative*, those who talk about the Soul, about Ideals? Ah! I was one of those. I *am* one of those, curse it. I have an imagination, it nestles deep within me like a well of unending water, and it is ever ready to flow over its

banks, to ooze everywhere, to colour everything with its wild
raiments of colour. Can you imagine what battle means to one
such as this? Can you imagine – try to imagine? Can you put
yourself in my place? Can you think of blood and bayonets
and explosions and men's entrails flying through the air –
"with the greatest of ease"?'

His voice was trembling now.

'Raymond,' said Frances sharply. 'Please stop talking like
this. You'll only upset Christine.'

'No, go on,' said Christine quietly. 'You're not upsetting me.
You make me feel I understand.'

'I do?' Raymond smiled, a wry hopeless smile. He shook his
head.

'No. No one can understand.' He looked out over the sea.
The sudden burst of words seemed to have left him denuded.
His voice sank to a whisper. 'Perhaps one could. A man called
Travers.'

'Raymond,' said Frances warningly.

He shrugged.

'Travers. A very ordinary man. An English name.' He turned
to Christine with an innocent, almost childlike look. 'He was
killed, you know. Killed in a field. By the Germans, officially.'

'There was a pause, as if Raymond was going to say
something else. He inclined his head to one side, stared out
again at the reservoir that might as well be the sea. Was it
France the other side, St Valéry and the woods, the farm? But
where were the goats? And the hills? God, was that the noise
again? – the drumming in his ears, the pounding at his chest,
the cold, cold fingers at his spine?

'No!' he exclaimed. 'No! No! No!'

And he held his hands up to his face, and shook with one,
two, three great unshed sobs.

'How can I make you understand? Never. Yet, you are a
writer. We share that in common. We love words, we know
what they can do. Can you understand – that in words I have
my only hope, my only prospect for the future?'

'Yes,' said Christine. 'That I believe is true.'

'But it has not come true,' said Raymond. 'That is the hell of it all. I can't write about the things that are deep in me, the horror and the filth and the hell of it. I can't put *them* into words. Every time I try, the words become tinny and brassy and tinkling – like some silly child's cymbals, clinking and clanking. How can I – I can't – I can't –'

Frances got to her feet, white and strained.

'Raymond, please pull yourself together. I want to talk to Christine. Will you see the children home?'

She bit her lip. At times like this, knowing in some intuitive way that Raymond was ever on the verge of some unimaginable catastrophe, she was frightened to leave the children with him. Yet she knew, too, that the children were his last link with any hope for the future. With the children, it seemed, he remained the old, the boyish Raymond, a man aloof from the shadow of the pit. That was why she took the risk, because she could not conceive what might happen otherwise.

'Don't let them be late for their tea, will you?' she said, and then she turned and picked up the picnic basket and motioned Christine to follow her.

*

For a time they walked in silence, Frances nibbling at a long blade of grass which she had snapped off angrily as she turned away from Raymond, Christine swinging her white summer hat from side to side, in her hand. They had so often in the past walked like this, Frances remembered, on those blessed Sunday afternoons at the boarding-school when you were 'free'. Free to hurry down to the town café and gorge cakes, to go and sit through blood-and-thunders in the tatty Palace cinema, or, as they usually did, to wander out on to the close-cropped winding Sussex downs – up and up until there was no higher part, only the helter-skelter wind and the smell of the sea blown in from the Channel. They were fourteen or fifteen, then, centuries ago, gangling schoolgirls hallmarked by their prim black stockings. Raymond was a blue-coated youth at a nearby public school; Oliver was – she supposed he was then starting at the agricultural college where his father insisted on sending him. Timothy and Theresa were, strange thought, without existence or shape, metaphysical elements. And now – she frowned.

They came into the north field, a mass of shy yellow.

'Oliver's experimenting here, a mustard crop.'

Down the side they went, avoiding treading on the delicate yellow-petalled plants. The next field sloped downwards to the wood.

'This is one of the cows' luncheon corners. They'll come here after Oliver and Mark have milked. They're good milkers – one gives an average of two gallons a day.'

They climbed over the stile and were suddenly in the cool shade of the wood. It was at once, as always, a private, personal place.

'It was strange you writing out of the blue like that,' Frances said. 'I think you are the one, the only possible person in the world, whom I would have wanted to see just now. Perhaps I'm deluding myself, perhaps we're really changed. But somehow I feel not. Though we had never met again, I think I would always have thought of you as if you were just round the corner, always my first and best friend. Gracious, doesn't that sound like something out of the fifth form?'

'Fourth form.' Christine raised her right hand and poked a finger thoughtfully at the rim of her hat. 'But it's funny you should say that. Because there was no specific reason why I should write you just this moment instead of, say, some other moment, a few weeks later, months even. And yet I felt quite definite about it.' She shrugged. 'Goodness knows why.'

They stopped in their tracks for a moment to watch an impudent jackdaw that was on the path ahead of them, preening itself and hopping about as if in sheer abandonment at being alive and awake on such a gloriously sharp spring day.

Frances sighed.

'Envious?'

'I think, quite a bit,' she said. 'I wouldn't mind changing places – for a while, anyway.'

Christine laughed.

'There's the real answer – "for a while". Which means, in effect, that you'd like to be free to dance around like the jackdaw, so long as you knew your nest was waiting for you to come back to when you were tired of dancing.'

Frances wrinkled her nose.

'I wonder if you're right. I don't know … Look, I don't want to spoil that lovely compliment you paid this afternoon,' she went on impulsively, 'because what you said is fundamentally true, it's what I've often, often felt. Especially when sometimes I've been away, or we've visited people in London. I've been appalled at the shallow, shiftless lives so many seem to lead. I've hated these smart women who "can't be bothered" to have children, and who think it's so sophisticated to live with a succession of different men … No, that only makes me wonderfully conscious of what a full and, well I suppose in many ways, enviable life I've had.'

'Oliver appears quite the ideal husband,' said Christine drily. 'And I'm not being sarcastic.'

'That's what I mean. Oliver. And the children. And here. I don't want you to think we're not, in so many ways, completely happy. I think – no, I know we are.' Frances paused, looking around at the green twisting undergrowth, the tall beech trees – but with vacant eyes. 'It's just that … Well, somehow, lately, I seem to feel restless all the time – sometimes quite irritated. As if in some subtle way I was being forced into a position that I felt was wrong. I – I – oh, you see, I can't even express it myself.'

'Try.'

'Well – well, look, for instance – Raymond. I'm dreadfully sorry about his behaviour. I can't expect you to understand having only met him for the first time. But he's really a sweet boy, and such an unhappy one. Of course, he must seem dreadfully neurotic, but he's not – well, yes, he is, but there are circumstances.'

'Obviously. He feels guilty about the war, I fancy.'

'Yes. But that's not the only thing.'

Christine nodded.

'I imagine the fundamental thing is his frustration as a writer?'

'Yes. I think so. Is it as obvious as that?'

Christine smiled.

'I doubt it. It's only because, as he said, we're both writers. To me, his feelings about his writing are written all over him. I've met many like him. They're at a cross-roads, and they know it, and they're secretly afraid they won't have the strength to go the right way. That's putting it all very allegorically, but that's roughly it.'

'And Raymond – does he strike you as one of the successful ones? I don't mean successful in the commercial sense.'

Christine laughed.

'My dear, Raymond could never be successful in the commercial sense because no one with any feeling and sensitivity can be so hard and ruthless and – well, business-minded – to succeed commercially. I have quite a task myself, and you know I'm no starry-eyed innocent.'

'But still, do you think –'

'Darling, I hardly know Raymond.'

'I'm asking you.'

'Well.' Christine frowned. 'Let me answer with a question – what do you think?'

Frances hesitated.

'If I were honest, I would say I think sometimes that Raymond is in the grip of some evil process of events, like a spiral whirlpool – but a process that he almost manufactures himself. And when I think that, I can't believe that he will ever escape – that the end is – is –'

'I think that's enough about Raymond,' said Christine swiftly, 'because, however fond of him you are, he's not your real problem? Or is he?'

'Well, only partly.' Frances felt a layer of shyness melting, felt the old intimacy binding them together. Impulsively she took Christine's elbow.

'It is good ... to be able to talk. There's been no one I could talk to. Sometimes I've lain awake thinking and thinking ... Sometimes I've wished it were something easy and conventional, Oliver being unfaithful, for instance. Does that shock you?'

'Not at all. I can see already that it wouldn't matter – that it wouldn't alter your marriage fundamentally.'

'Oh, yes, that's true. I'm sure about Oliver and me, that we have made a whole life together, and that we shall always be together. And yet. And yet …'

She paused, aghast – and yet what? How could she even capture into words what she hardly knew, such intangibility? How could she be sure that her sense of grievance was legitimate, was not merely a cloak for selfishness?

Her hands fluttered helplessly in front of her, beating and probing at the air as if trying to fashion out of it some shape of her thoughts. Watching her Christine was reminded of an image of some lovely and graceful bird, a thing of stately, serene beauty, suddenly halted in its flight. She felt an unsuspected rush of tenderness for this girl – and in some way she still retained the freshness of a girl – with whom she had shared the formative, exciting years of her own life. She knew that what she had said was true, that Frances had found her true path in life; yet she also understood – and her professional pride was annoyed that she had not at once perceived this – that there was now for Frances some crisis, some unavoidable knot which must be cut. As to the nature of it she remained uncertain, but of the probable solution, the way out and at once the way forward, she already had a shrewd idea.

'You see,' said Frances with deliberation, 'for years now I've been a sort of centrepiece, the pin around which the wheel revolves – oh, I'm not being conceited or romantic, that's how it has been. Oliver, the children, then Raymond – they all turn to me, they all come to me, they all, in a way, make demands on me …' She paused, feeling as always a shameful sense of how plaintive and petulant it must sound, wishing she could make someone else see it as she now felt it, convincingly.

'It's something that has not seemed a problem before. Perhaps the fault is mine, perhaps I'm tired or something – but no, in my heart I know it has no accidental explanation. I know, in my heart, that both Oliver and Raymond are leaning on me – you might say clinging – and using me for sustenance, and – and –'

'Taking you for granted?'

Frances smiled wryly.

'Perhaps ... Perhaps there's something of that in it. But what I'm trying to get at is – it's in the *wrong* way – it's being done selfishly. Any woman would be only too proud and happy to give her husband her strength and love. But somehow, lately, it seems to me that this is almost outside Oliver's perception. Sometimes I feel I have become something automatic, a unit, in the pattern of his life. That I, and the children, are all part of a pattern with only one purpose, the fulfilment of his ambitions. And in many ways he's an extremely ambitious man, you know.'

'It's not a bad quality.'

'But surely, on its own, for its own sake, it is? And now, though I try to fight against it, I find myself wondering how much Oliver is in love with ambition for its own sake. It's a curious, involved thing. It's not that he's ambitious to be a Prime Minister or a film star or anything fantastic. It's merely that he seems to care more for the feeling of achieving, of progressing, of in some way or other gaining more power – than, well for anything else. It's when I feel like that, and know how he is always turning to me to get his strength and comfort – it's then that something seems to shrivel inside me, something seems to close up and not want to give, not want to be used in such a mechanical way.'

Frances sighed. 'How helpless I am at describing it. I wish I had your gift of words. It sounds nonsense the way I say it. After all, you're probably thinking, he is her husband. That's her job, helping him to get on. Oh, it's more than that, I do assure you, Christine, dear – and it's worse because I feel it's only come about lately. Those early years, those glorious years when we started out, and built up things – here, the farm, the home, then the children, a family, seeing it grow – everything seems to be unquestioned, we were working together. We achieved because achievements were part of the pattern of a family growing. But now, somehow, it's different ... The farm is successful, we could sit back and enjoy life, there are other things besides the farm. But Oliver seems to get obsessed with expanding, expanding, expanding – buying more land, farming bigger farms, making more money. And I know it's not for our sakes – not even for his own sake as far as comfort goes. No, it's to satisfy some sort of craving. Oh, Christine, it frightens me almost ...'

'I know, Frances, I can see how it must. But –'

'But!' exclaimed Frances in a sudden passion. 'How I hate that word. How much and how little it can mean. And how many times I say it to myself – *but* Oliver's a good kind husband, *but* this, *but* that, *but* you're in love with Oliver. Oh yes, I'm in love with Oliver, I know that, but – that word again! *but* I know too there's a part of me, a loving part, that is finding no expression – that despite myself won't emerge – and *that* is the trouble I'm sure. I'm not being – well, to use one of your women's magazine phrases – I'm not being my true self.'

'And I suppose you feel the same with Raymond?'

'Yes. All my life I've had to mother him, look after him, give him re-assurance. And it's wrong, I feel it's wrong.'

Frances swallowed hard. 'Oh, I feel so mean talking to you like this. But I have this constant feeling, that it can't go on, that – that –'

Christine took her arm gently, guiding her down the path towards the orange-gold blob where the wood ended.

'How will it all end? What will happen? Christine, sometimes I'm frightened ... to think of hurting anyone.'

Christine tightened her grip.

'Dearest Frances, it's not for me to say what will happen. I'm a woman like you, and that's perhaps why everything you say is quite clear to me. To a man perhaps it would be incomprehensible.' She laughed. 'At all events, a man wouldn't like it. I suppose you've tried to talk to Oliver?'

'Yes. But it's difficult. And we've never got very far with it.'

'Darling, as I say, it's a problem you must work out yourself. That's perhaps cold comfort for you – but I'm sure you know in your heart it's all I could say.'

They came to the stile at the other end of the path, clustered around with hanging willow leaves.

'And if you insist on my saying something, Frances, I will –

that if you're *not* being your true self you simply must become it. What that involves I can only guess, and perhaps you hardly know yourself. But I do think, I'm sure, that in the end there'll be no loss for anyone – everyone will gain. And if that sounds a paradox to you, well –'

Christine pushed back the hazy shadow of hanging branches and revealed the open sky and the long grassy slopes.

'– again as the women's magazines would certainly say, that's life, sister.'

But going forward out of the clinging wood into the generous sunshine, Frances felt a sudden relief, conscious that the mere fact of being able to speak to someone had removed some almost unbearable load – and, in some way, that the pattern had resolved itself one step further.

*

At dinner that night they sat in the hall, around the old circular oak table that (so legend had it) had groaned under many wonderful banquets of old, and had once drawn the attendance of the great Richard Grenville. The table was stained here and there with dark patches, and it was easy to imagine each one as the symbol of some momentous gathering, some extra gay and timeless occasion; this one where the reigning lord of the manor had always set down his wine goblet, that one where the fat had dripped off the spoked roast lamb – and this wandering black vein where the blood had spurted out of the angry plunge of a dagger into some velvet-plumed heart. It was Raymond who pointed them out, one by one, elaborating upon the legends, adorning each one with unexpected flashes of description. Momentarily he seemed to step away from himself into new garments; his eyes flashed, his face lit up, there was a surge of vitality about him that communicated itself and swept them away.

Ah, Raymond, my dearest, if only this was you always, if only this was your harmony and not your wayward clasping at a dream, thought Frances. Her heart cried out at the anguish of the unachievable. She sat there with her eyes on him, wanting to give him such a shock of warmth and strength that he would outgrow himself; would become, despite himself, what she had once thought he would become. But even as she willed and prayed, even then there was a tell-tale crack in his voice, there was the imperceptible pause, the beginnings of a ramble – the signs that she knew deep in the echoes of her heart were the true ones – and she knew now, as they would know a moment later, that the spark would peter out and Raymond would sit through the rest of the meal in a sudden torture of moodiness.

And yet it was an occasion of natural gaiety that forced itself upon them. It was something, one of those rare happenings that had been awaited with pleasant anticipation, that had come to fruition, and that would remain as a memory of sustenance and renewal. It was 'the week-end that Christine came'. About it there might seem nothing extraordinary, just a visit from some sophisticated outer world into the narrowed circle of their own seasonal rhythm. Yet the contact, as with all contacts of opposites, had fired and aroused, had renewed.

'Christine, I'm sure I should be considerably antipathetic to your writings,' said Oliver pleasantly, carving the chicken breast in delicate slices. 'So you'll realise that when I ask you the favour of sending me a copy of your latest book you're being paid a very great compliment.'

'For certain you are,' said Frances, 'considering Oliver never reads a novel from one end of the year to the other.'

'Flattered I'm sure,' laughed Christine. 'I shall send you one as soon as I get back. And I shall inscribe it, too.'

'How?'

'Ah, just you wait. Words that will bring shame to your un-literary heart.'

'If I were you, Christine, I should inscribe it: To A Man Who Married His Farm and Works At Being Husband,' said Frances. Tonight, in this mood, it was teasing, a bit of laughter: another time it might have sounded bitter.

'Ah, you see, Christine, she's jealous.'

Oliver replied banteringly, too, and the bitterness of himself remained also tucked far away.

Yet it is there, deep down, saw Christine, through the pleasant layer of companionship. But just because there was that layer, she knew the conflict did not matter that evening. She knew, as they knew, that her visit had been opportune, had provided a link, perhaps a junction, a starting point or a departure point.

The curious thing was how much she had herself extracted from the week-end. How good it had been for her to come. Lately she had felt a sense of superficiality and drifting in her own life, of the whole of life around her. She had lived too long in the dried air of central heating and tube stations, of hothouse flats and lifts and automatic living. She had felt a sense of release as soon as she had stepped out of the car into the night that surrounded, so vastly and generously, the quiet country landscape, the solitary farmhouse. She had felt, as her nerves had not allowed her to feel for months, able to relax completely, to drop the weary mask of high-pressure living, to become simple again.

And here there were the elements of what she knew now she was looking for herself – here had been fashioned the roots of a life that was real. The undercurrent of restlessness and of unease did not alter this. It was curious how true was that truism, that an outsider was able to see things much more clearly than a participant. She saw herself as some ghost-like stranger standing on the edge of their lives, seeing the routes and the procedures so clearly, so accurately. What she had told Frances was quite true, though she did not expect Frances to believe it at this moment. For she, Christine, had felt at once the sense of a pattern about this house, about its life and its future. In that pattern she saw room for upheavals, and for sorrows, as well as triumphs and laughter – death, perhaps, as well as life. But with an odd perception, she knew there could be, would be, no break, and no end to the pattern.

So she looked at Frances with affection and was happy to have come at a right moment, to have been able to give her friend that sustenance which it is the great joy and privilege of friendship to give. And because she had given it of herself and without thought, so was she herself fulfilled, and would return to London the next day a happier woman.

Oh yes, I see how well you understand your friend, Frances, how one woman understands another woman, deep into their inner secrets, thought Raymond, looking across the table, between two graciously parting daffodils – looking at Christine's serene face and wise eyes of a woman of the world. But what do you know of a man's world that is so many continents apart from a woman's? What can you know of my world that has never been and that only floats among the cosmos in disintegrating spirals? – that has no physical body and shape, yet can be as real. What do you know of the haunted chambers beating with the flutter of wings that are resounding here within me, he thought wildly – and suddenly he beat his fist on his chest as if to banish them, knowing it was futile.

And then seized the wine glass and stood up, holding it to the light so that the white wine sparkled like the sun, and gave a toast.

'Here's to Christine, and here's to Frances, and here's to Oliver – and here's to Raymond! And may we fulfil all our years and our months and our weeks and our hours, and our triumphant destinies!'

They were startled and even frightened for a moment, but the wine inside them was warming and uplifting and they stood up and drank and laughed, and drank again, and were united in the exhilaration.

But afterwards when the food was finished and they were smoking and drinking, when the table was resplendent with the evidence of the good food and the contented diners, Frances felt a stab, as of some stranger's sword, across the smooth shield of her contentment. It is wrong, she thought. I will not open my mind to it, she thought. And she clung to the mirror reflection of their happiness and contentment. But despite herself the sword pierced again and again ... and she was remembering standing in the little hut and looking at the portrait of Mark, the strangeness of the hands; remembering him framed in the doorway, filling it with sunshine and life, and walking alongside her across the fields and the music of his voice in its gentle hesitancy.

But why must I think of Mark, she asked herself in the trouble of her heart. And looked at Oliver, with his cheeks flushed and his eyes aglow, as he talked of his immense plans for developing the farm into three separate farms, later into an agricultural estate – but got no answer from her look. Why, she asked. And looked at Raymond, his eyes peering into the shadows and the mists, over horizons that she could not even see and that might never exist, yet must exist or else he was the lost soul – but found no answer. Oh why, she asked. And looked at Christine and saw her face grave and reposed, her hair curled in gentle spirals up the back of her neck, leaving the nape white and virgin-like, her body held erect and dignified, and saw Christine not only as another woman but as all women, each having the problems of all and of each other – and perhaps in the straight body and implicit integrity of Christine, and the flashing memory of that text-book slogan 'To thine own self be true', she saw the framework into which she must secretly fit her answer.

And abruptly she got up, on the pretext of clearing the table. When she was alone in the kitchen she took a tray and laid a plate on it, heaped with the delicacies remaining: some salad, two slices of chicken, roast potatoes, brown bread and butter and a cut of the rich fruit cake. She filled up one of the wine glasses and perched it in a corner; then, taking down a torch, she went through the back door and across the dark yard, and out into the night covering the field and the tiny waiting light.

She was breathing quickly by the time she reached the door, her arms weary from the weight of the tray, but she had not spilled a drop. She could not knock so she called out softly. She heard him moving, and the door opening.

'Why –' he began, and retreated. 'But do come in.'

'I will come in just to put this tray down.'

She stood in the centre of the tiny room, absorbing the scene: the little lantern on the shelf by the bed, the small pile of books, one open where he was reading – the tiny oil stove in the corner. The room had a warmth that was lacking in the daytime, and it was made whole and human by his presence, by seeing him in all his solitude.

'I will put it here, on this little table.'

Quickly he moved a packet of cigarettes and some matches, and she put the tray down.

He looked at it with pleasure, yet shyly.

'Really, it is good of you.'

She stood ill at ease, looking away from him.

'I don't quite know – oh, I was sitting there, we were having a farewell meal before my friend went. I tried not to think about it but I saw you sitting here so alone ...'

She saw him stiffen, and involuntarily stretched a hand out to touch his arm.

'Oh, please, don't – don't think I am doing it out of pity, because I am sorry for you. That would not be fair, and it would not be true.'

Gently he took her hand, held it for a moment, then dropped it.

'It is quite all right. I know it is not pity. I know –' he paused, groping for the right word and feeling awkward because he could not find it – 'because one knows these things.'

'Yes,' she said eagerly. For the fraction of a second she turned to him and their eyes met.

'I must go back or they will – I must go back now.'

She turned and opened the door. He made no move to follow her. When she turned he had sat down on the bed and was watching her. His eyes were open and unscreened, revelatory. She looked back wonderingly, a little afraid.

'Good night,' he said softly.

'Good night,' she whispered.

And then she was gone, out into the darkness, leaving him sitting a long, long time on his bed, watching the flickering of the lamp and the dull red glow of the oil stove, and, lastly, the neat, almost loving array of the food and the wine – until a tiny smile played at his lips and grew over his face, wiping away the tiredness, and all at once he looked exactly as he looked in the portrait that had been painted so many unbelievable years ago, in that age of forgotten happiness.

When she was back she made up a tray of coffee and walked in with it, and there was no suspicion only a gay welcome awaiting, so that the evening bubbled on and died away in a gentle peace and contentment, until they all went up the side stairs to their sleeps and dreams. That night, because her body was warm and gently awoken, she turned to Oliver as one suddenly possessed of an emormous generosity and they were happy and fulfilled in the darkness, as it is possible to be in the detached world of the night, remote from realities and problems. But he, as well as she, was aware of the subtle flaw, of a prelude instead of an epilogue: and it was as much this wandering troubled thought as the glasses of rich wine that left his sleep faintly disturbed and the night an uneasy respite.

V

Oliver started ploughing into the jungle soon after daybreak. What he always referred to as the jungle was the several acres of unkempt, overgrown land which he had bought with the farmhouse when they first came there, ten years ago. At first the whole farm, even the kitchen garden, had been like this, sheer wild jungle; tangled roots, stumps of trees, rabbit burrows, everywhere the virulent groping fingers of grassweed. That had been, for him, the tremendous attraction, as much as it was a challenge. He would have been a little lost if his life had been without this permanent challenge, this taunt to his ambition.

From his earliest years he had been determined that when he became a farmer in his own right it would not be at second-hand, he would do more than merely pay down a pile of banknotes to acquire some neat, ticking-over property which needed no more than to be kept dutifully in order. No, he would seek out land that had gone back to the wild, untamed stage, land that cried out to be grappled with and tamed, coaxed back to its natural fertility. Tregonna had been exactly the place he required. The big stone farmhouse, solid and comfortable enough for living in; the scruffy sides of the valley, rough and wild enough to challenge all the latent energy and pride seeded within him.

They had begun as now he was carrying on, first clearing the foliage, then re-tracing the ancient hedges and ditches, then hiring a tractor and rumbling backwards and forwards with a great iron plough plunging and bucking behind. There had been no thrill to compare with the one on that day when at last the first field was ploughed and harrowed, and re-ploughed and planted with corn. He had found a deep satisfaction in watching the neat purposeful cuts of the plough, like lines of a man's life – all his creation, out of his mind and performed with his hands and his toil. There had been other thrills: each time the land reclamation was repeated, each time they cut another field out of its cloak of forgotten time and sloth, each time the brushwood and the weeds and the scrub-heaps were banished and the ancient, ever fertile dark soil, studded with the clear white stones so common to the district, was turned up to the kiss of the weather.

Now, looking down the growing ladder of years, it seemed they had done an enormous amount, fashioning an entire farm out of the jungle, one, two, three, four, five – altogether eight fields. But to stand on top of Tinker's Hill and look west and east was to tuck the achievement away into memory and be imbibed with the exhilaration of a new challenge – acres and acres that lay waiting, expectant, difficult for wooing like a new love yet as potential of richness and fertility.

Now it was his own tractor, a fiery red Fordson, that he drove out of the yard and across the mist-flavoured fields toward the distant line of stubble and bracken. And now, savouring their adventurous ride on the tractor, it was his own children in their bright sweaters, who flaunted before him like two ripe plants out of some harvest. His own son, hair blowing in the wind, blue eyes flashing with great fires of inner excitement, his own son riding out with him on the adventure; a son who would some day continue, as the crops continued one after another, season in and out. And so he had yet another reason to add to the many that made him drive on and on like someone possessed, like some victorious general pushing steadily into enemy country, yet always knowing – and half desiring – that there were more enemies lying ahead.

He saw no limit to that drive. His mind envisaged some day that the farm should have grown until it was a vast estate. In his more grandiose moments he saw it assuming the shape and dignity and proportions of something more than a farm, rather more like one of the old feudal estates. To achieve so much hadn't been easy, he thought, whining up the tractor engine and slipping in the clutch, tumbling out of the yard gate and on to the rough churned-up mud and grassland. It wasn't, indeed, only the land he had to fight, nor only the weather with its treachery and flashy promises. There were other oppositions. Local farmers scoffed at his madhat schemes for land reclamation – the Cornish farm labourers, tradition-bound, were inclined to be unsympathetic because he was a stranger and they somehow resented his intrusion even while ready to pocket his money. Well, he had faced all the attacks, all the treacheries and betrayals. And there was only one way to do that, to ensure your own continuity and life, and that was to put on armour, to cling to your purposes and intentions stubbornly, and if necessary ruthlessly.

He was proud because he had achieved what he had set out to achieve, and proud because he knew he would achieve what he still intended to achieve – more reclamation, increased fertility, the farm swelling and swelling. It was odd, sometimes it was his most bitter and frustrating enemy, yet he believed passionately in the land, and its place as the root of human happiness. He could never be happy working in a city. His idea of a private hell was the electric lighting and metallic humming of a factory bench. He felt, quite genuinely, a supreme satisfaction and peace when he was out in the fields with the soil crumbling under his feet and the elements, wet or fine, wrapped around him with the fresh touch of eternal virginity.

But not being a poet or a writer he could not express what he felt, except in his own way of action.

'All right, Timmy? All right, Terry? Then here we go.'

They had crossed the two west fields. Now he swung the tractor sharply through the farthest gateway and they were at the beginning of the new field. He ground the tractor to a standstill and left the engine throbbing over, little jets of smoke puffing up as if from someone's pipe.

'My!' cried Timothy excitedly. 'Will this be the terminus?'

'That's right, Timmy. Journey's end – at least for the joy ride. Now we start work.'

Timothy danced beside the huge rubber wheel.

'I can work too, can't I?'

'Silly,' sniffed Theresa. 'You're not big enough.'

'I am, I am, aren't I, Daddy? I can work – I can drive a tractor.'

Oliver grinned down at the eager upturned face, seeing in it a hundred reflections of his own. Except that, he remembered, his own eagerness had so often been thwarted or in some subtle way dampened when he was a child – not completely, perhaps not even deliberately, but enough to leave him with the canker of resentment. Well, Timothy would be spared that if he could help it.

'Of course you can work, old lad. Anyway, I hear from Uncle Raymond you make a very good general.'

'That's right, Daddy. I captured the German field-marshal.'

'*We* did,' said Theresa hotly. 'I was Mata Hari, Daddy, that was what really did it.'

'Well, anyway we did it.'

'Well done,' said Oliver. 'I think a successful general ought to make a good farmer's assistant.' He pretended to look down gravely. 'I tell you what – here's a job for you both. While Daddy drives the tractor up and down I want you both to walk behind – keep a good way behind though – and tell Daddy if the plough isn't going straight, will you?'

'Yes, Daddy. Yessir.'

He straightened out in the tractor seat, revved up the engine, and let in the clutch.

'Here we go then!'

With a grunt the tractor met the first impact as the steel plough bit into the hard ground. The week before he and Mark and Raymond had spent hours hacking and clearing the undergrowth and levelling out, but still the uncovered land would fight tenaciously against the invasion. It would be a long and stubborn battle, the long morning and afternoon – perhaps most of the evening – before the task was finished. But he knew, sitting there, a straight, firm, rather lonely figure, the peaked cap pulled down to shade the sun from his eyes, his mouth closed in a firm line, his jaw jutting out slightly towards the waiting jungle – he knew the job would be done.

'Watch that plough, workers,' he called over his shoulder almost merrily. Then his eyes were glued on the imaginary track ahead of him.

'Yessir, yessir. Watching the line.'

And Timothy and Theresa marched sturdily in his wake. Theresa stepping a little daintily as befitting a gentle and to-be-beautiful lady, Timothy treading with the solid plod of the countryman born and dedicated – his short pants blowing out in the breeze and his dark hair falling over his eyes, a strange feeling of contentment in his bones that he would never be able to express for many years to come.

*

After the milking was over that evening Mark came through the yard and round to the back door. He carried under his arm the two books he had borrowed the previous day. He read quickly, at least one book an evening, sometimes two. He liked to get into the bed and fix the lantern at his side, on the upturned box, and to read on and on while his body was tucked securely into the warmth. He read avidly and intently because it was sheer enjoyment to do so; yet also, he knew, because the quicker he read, the quicker he could take the books and go again to the tall house and the quiet, shadowy library – and Frances.

She was alone in the kitchen when he came. She watched his head bobbing along the screen of the window, and knew a familiar moment of tenseness before his knock echoed on the door. It was the third day of his coming, and already it was as much expected by her as by him.

'Good evening. I have come with the books, thank you.'

'I hope you enjoyed them?'

'Very much. You have such nice books.'

He smiled and she noticed his unconscious habit of half closing one eye as he did, lending him an air of whimsicality that probably he did not possess.

'I am very grateful to be able to borrow them.'

'You know you're welcome,' she said and motioned him to follow her through to the library.

The room was bathed with a rich golden light from the sun, now tucking down towards the horizon. The rays fell across the red and black and green leather backs of the books, seeming to emphasise their colours, giving the room an unexpected warmth and brightness. On the table was a single bowl of rich red tulips that he had gathered that morning from the garden. In the corner was the silent writing desk where she, sometimes, Raymond more often would sit and write. And in the furthest corner, unfamiliarly spotlighted in the tip of the sunshine, was the black baby grand piano that had come to them as a legacy.

She was surprised to feel Mark stiffen at her side, overcome by some constraint so strong that she could feel it in her own body.

'Why – what is it?'

She saw that he had turned quite pale, and she noticed again how long his arms were and the curious way in which they were suddenly stretched forward, as if reaching out.

'A piano. You have a piano.'

His voice was unexpectedly dulled.

'Oh, of course. It's always been covered up – I suppose you didn't notice it. I took away the cover this morning to have it cleaned. Alas, none of us here plays.'

She paused, hearing his short uneven breathing.

'Do you?'

And as she spoke, letting her glance at the same time drop casually to his hands, she knew suddenly – and the knowledge came to her with force as being of great importance – she knew that he did play.

He looked across at the piano, but without moving.

'I did play. A long time ago.'

'Oh!' She was aware of a need for delicacy in choice of words. 'You played a lot? Professionally?'

'I played – professionally.'

He was taut and bound up. She expected no more, perhaps only a silence. It was what he intended. He had no intention of collapsing so suddenly the prison bars with which he had surrounded himself and his hands for those four years. But it was something beyond him, something intangible save that it was, he supposed, bound up with a wisp of fair hair curling out of place, with the long white curve of her neck, with the sheer warmth of a woman, this woman, beside him, impregnating him with her aliveness.

Whatever it was he felt the hot tears leaping up, spouting out like animals suddenly released from cages, pouring over the dry country of his cheeks.

'I'm sorry,' he muttered. 'Forgive me. I'm sorry.'

He took a step forward and then, helplessly, he ran forward to the piano and half collapsed on to the stool, burying his hands to his face upon the closed piano lid. It was in some detached way theatrical, yet it was terrifyingly human.

She watched him go and she felt herself moving after him in a daze, aware with unbearable pain of all the years of suffering that lay deep behind those tears that had pierced and prodded, accumulated and hoarded, at last pouring out in those blind, hot, helpless tears.

She was standing above him. Gently she put a hand on his shoulder, touching it for him to know she was there, a reassurance.

'Tell me,' she said softly. 'That is, if you wish.'

'I am so sorry.' He raised his head but still look down at the black, shiny board. Over his shoulder she could see the reflection of his face.

'I had no idea. You must excuse ... It was a sudden shock. I had not seen a piano for a long time. To tell you the truth, I forced myself not to see them. I had almost come to believe there were not such things ... a stupid thought, is it not?'

He laughed.

'For me, a very stupid thought.'

He looked down at his hands, now hardened from farm work, as if seeking to penetrate to the delicacy and softness of touch that had once been there.

'My father was a musician, a pianist, but not as you would say, a professional. Perhaps he might have been a very great pianist, but the circumstances of his life did not allow that. My

father was a poor man, he had to struggle hard for a living –
and there was something he loved even more than music. That
was my mother – later the children. It was to them that his life
was firstly dedicated. It was for them he worked and slaved,
determined that they should never want, that they should have
the comforts and freedom that he always lacked.

'And how my father worked ... He was a printer. I
remember how he used to come home late at night, weary and
red-eyed. For years he was a compositor, straining his eyes to
read indecipherable writing, to see the types. Always straining.
And although eventually he launched on his own as a little
jobbing printer, I don't think he ever recovered from the strain
of those years. When I last saw him, just after the war broke out
he was very tired and his eyesight was failing rapidly.'

Mark pressed his hands together carefully.

'And yet, you understand, he was a happy man. He would
have died a happy man because he and my mother remained in
love all their lives. And if he never fulfilled his own desires
about music, at least he perhaps did so through me. Yes ...'

He paused, and she felt his mind racing back over the years.
A tiny sigh escaped him.

'Perhaps in a way my father willed me into being a pianist. I
don't remember any special inclination towards music when I
was young. In fact the first time I can remember anything
specific I was about eight or nine, I suppose. I had come in
from school one afternoon and the door of our drawing-room
was ajar and I heard the sound of my mother singing. She had
a lovely crystal clear voice, rather weak, but extraordinarily
pure. I drew nearer. She was singing an old German folk song,
very softly. My father was accompanying her on the piano.
From where I was standing I saw through a slant in the
doorway, so that I could not see my mother, just the side of my
father and his hands moving over the keys. It was strange,
watching my father's hands moving up and down ... so gently,
so surely ... and as I stood there watching it was almost as if I
felt rather than heard the song and the music, felt it all through
my father's hands with their gentle caressing of the keys.'

Mark shrugged.

'This must sound rather exaggerated to you.'

'No, no, it doesn't. Please go on.'

'I think it was from that moment that I felt myself drawn to music. Perhaps my father sensed this. At any rate he began giving me lessons on the piano. Later he sent me to a special teacher. I don't know quite how it all happened, I'm not conscious of having worked terribly hard but somehow I seemed to have a natural talent for the piano.'

He looked at his hands again, stretching out each finger as if recovering some old habit dimly remembered.

'And so, eventually, my father saved up the money to send me to Heidelberg. Ah, yes, you would like Heidelberg with its winding streets and its beautiful old buildings. At least, you would have liked it. I suppose now they are all in ruins.'

'And then what happened?' prompted Frances.

'And then? I studied, one year, two years – I made progress. I gave my first recital. A great occasion! My father was there in a seat of honour ... he was so happy that night, he and my mother. And there were other recitals. I finished my studies, another three years. I was complimented by Weingartner himself. He said I had a brilliant career ahead of me. I already had been invited to play at Munich, at Berlin, at Hamburg. There was even talk of going to France.'

Mark swung round on the piano stool until he was facing out of the window, out to the red rimming sun.

'You see, I was rather like that sun is – not now, but early in the morning, when it stands on the threshold of the day. And then, all at once, there was war – a war I had little knowledge or feeling for – but nevertheless, a war. And so, now I feel rather more like the sun as it is there, dying, dying, dying.'

He sighed.

'A few weeks after I was called up from the reserve I was shipped out to Libya. I was captured at Benghazi. From that day until now I have never been near a piano – have never, with the exceptions of glimpses through a window, seen a piano. Now there is one here beside me I no longer trust my eyes.

'I will not believe it until I touch, until my fingers feel and know,' he said, and his hands groped along the edges and lines of the piano.

He dropped his hands and hung his head. Between them there was an enormous void of silence in which she could almost hear their hearts beating.

'I don't know what made me – talk like this. I haven't said a word to anyone. It has been four years.'

She waited compassionately for him to finish all that he wanted to say, for the bottle to be drained.

'Or perhaps I do know,' he said with unexpected directness. 'It is because in some way you have entered my life and I have entered yours, and there has been made a pathway out of the prison, is it not?'

And now she was sorry that she had waited for him to go on. Yet, in the same moment, secretly, glad.

'You mustn't talk like that,' she said hastily. 'You mustn't.'

'But you don't deny it?'

She went and stood by the window. The sun was half hidden behind the ridge. The sun that was dying, dying, dying.

'Oh, promise me,' she said swinging round. 'Promise me, now you have found this piano – promise that you will play again?'

He looked at her slowly, for a long moment. She felt his eyes somehow drawing her into him.

'I will promise. Yes. Now I feel a freedom, now I feel a new hope. I will promise.'

And with those words he swung back to the piano and, with a decisive movement, opened the lid to expose the shiny line of polished keys.

As he did so Frances walked quickly across the room.

'Please play,' she said quietly. 'And I will see that you are left undisturbed.'

'Oh, but' – he paused with his hands in mid-air, bending forward as if eager to touch – 'I want you to stay and listen. I want to play to you.'

She flushed, standing with her hand on the door.

'No. I have to go. But I want you to play.'

He inclined his head.

'Very well. You shall leave me alone. And I shall play. But remember, I am playing to you. I shall play for you only.'

She had gone through the door, closing it gently behind her, and was taking her third step away across the hall when she heard the first notes ringing out, a strange harsh chord as if chosen to rend the peaceful air and silence, as if to declare fiercely that here was a purpose and a declaration.

She stood irresolute in the middle of the hall, half listening to the silence that hung about the rest of the house, half listening to the unfamiliar music. She had a strange sense of the house and its contents being wrapped up in some eternal moment that had brought time to a standstill. She remembered that the house was empty and devoid of humanity except for herself and Mark in the library; that Oliver and the children would be down in the fields another two hours, that Raymond had gone into Bedruthan, that Edith had gone home.

She remembered the other evening when she had stood restlessly in the hallway, the evening when the wind had blown about the house like an ominous intruder, and it seemed to her that this was that evening again, only brought to fruition. She had known then that there was a mystery and a confusion. She knew now that there was no mystery, only a hesitation.

And not wishing to admit the knowledge, she forced herself to stir, to move about the house as she had done the other evening. She walked up the stairs, avoiding looking into the mirror; went up to see that the children's bedroom was tidy and ready for them. She opened doors and looked into rooms and shut the doors again and walked away. And all the time, wherever she went, the sound of the piano music below followed her. It seemed to her as she listened that the note of the music reflected a mood, that it had changed from the soft and caressing notes which had followed the opening bars, that it had now become dominant and demanding, triumphal. Hearing, she turned away, as if in a vain attempt to drown the sound. But now it seemed to grow louder and louder, until it travelled over the whole house, until it filled the room where she stood.

And, staring ahead of her into the dusk, she thought she could suddenly see the faint white outline of Mark's hands, as she had seen them on the picture, as she had seen them held out towards her downstairs. They had become hypnotic hands, they rose and fell if they were waves, and her eyes rose and fell with them. Through the hands she felt music, the sound of running mountain streams, of chanting winds that travelled through long forests, of water lapping in a lake. And now, as the music seemed to flood every corner of the room and of her being, now she thought the hands grew larger and larger and came nearer and nearer; until they encompassed her, and she felt her body submerge into an enveloping warmth; until she was no longer a separate decisive entity, no longer herself, but belonging to the music and therefore to the hands.

It was then that she found she had turned back from the window where she had been standing, and that she was walking towards the door. She walked slowly and carefully, without any sense of surprise, almost with resignation. Yet she walked without hesitation. There was no longer any unwillingness. She knew that she would walk down the stairs and across the hall and up to the door of the library, and that she would enter …

The music stopped, cut off brusquely, hands left curved above the keys: not in surprise, but in welcome.

'You have come,' he said, simply.

'Yes.'

Then he played on, but now gently, now tenderly and delicately. And as he played she came slowly across the room and stood hear him, beside him, looking down at his playing. She had the awareness of something binding them suddenly, like a rope; of the rope being his hands, and that now she moved with every one of the hands' movements. She moved with the running fingers, she moved with the static chords. The hands, from the disappearing darkness above the wrists down to the white fleshy fingertips, were alive and she was alive with them. She felt pain, and there were strange achings in her arms and in her feet, and up and down her spine. She felt pleasure, and her whole body tingled, she breathed more heavily, more sensuously, and the taste of her mouth went sweet.

And all at once there grew up an unbearable tension, a taut stretch of the rope, a pressing together of dark heavy eyelids with the screeching pain of the unbearable. All her confusions were pounding around her head like great hammers, all her frustration and disappointment, all her inexplicable restlessness. There was a great sea of weight pressing down upon her … Suddenly there was an explosion, a flash of pure light.

And it was she, gently, who put her hand on his head and slid it down to his neck and then sank, without surprise, into the two arms that pulled her round and down into the long, awaited embrace.

*

Later that evening, when the moon was up, Raymond came down the stairs quietly and slipped out of the back door without the others noticing. He had been in his room ever since returning from Bedruthan, building himself a neat fire of wood logs and sitting in front of it, holding out his arms to the quickly devouring flames and watching their image curl around his silhouetted fingers. He sat in the only seat in the room, a deep wicker armchair, and the only sound was the slight squeak as he gently rocked backwards and forwards. The light from the Aladdin lamp on the mantelpiece threw a pale semi-circle around the chair, focusing it like some strange exhibit, some alien part of the room that was silhouetted for the gaping and guffawing of a hidden, hostile audience. All this he pretended not to notice so long as he stared downwards, into the impenetrable heart of the fire. But as soon as he looked up, or outwards, he was painfully conscious of this sense of his solitude, his alienation even from the objects in his own room. The fire was the only single living thing that gave him some warmth, and, he thought bitterly, it was something he had to make and create himself, that would quickly die without his constant attention.

He had felt alone and empty that evening, up in the room, but had forced himself to sit there, forced himself to ignore the cold insolent glare of the light, to ignore the sense of dancing shadows, of strangers gathering around him, menacing strangers, of whole worlds tumbling upon him of which he was ignorant. Until he could bear it no longer, kicking the chair back, flinging himself away from the fire, the light, the shadows – away, away, anywhere to get away from the solitary madness; down, down, the stairs and into the cloak of the night.

He walked with quick nervous strides, holding his body taut as if embarked on some urgent, purposeful journey, whereas in fact he had no purpose and no need of haste. He crossed the home field and then turned right and along the hedge path leading over to the reservoir. It was as if, quite unconsciously, the water hypnotised him. It was an age-old struggle in his life. He was frightened of water. He could never look at a silent pool and marvel at its placidness. He saw the pool when a stone had dropped heavily in the centre and thick frowning lines were spreading over its face, distorting and transfiguring it into something evil – a black yawning heart, alive with lurking shadows, beneath the glassy mask. When he was a child and sat gazing at the shimmer of a holiday summer sea he saw it as a mirage, the white crests of occasional foam as the warning freckles of hidden octopus mouths. He walked down to the wet path of the sands and felt himself treading on the blood of a thousand drowned men and a thousand drowned women. He sickened within himself as he looked at the smirking bubbles of foam, he trembled at the thought of the waves that had been split by frantic hands and then closed like iron trap-doors. And on stormy mornings he crept down in the dawn and saw the sea without its mask, saw the snarling, lashing flickering waves bursting in all their fury on the battered sands, spitting their blood and their hatred across the pebbled beaches. Once, frenzied and gripping his heart in a tight fist, he strode through the shallow sands with blood beating in his head and ringing in his ears and stared straight into a million beady eyes of the towering sea and spat his hate and defiances. But his voice sounded like a grass weed whistling in the breeze and choked in mid-air. A bitter wind flaked with the seaweed tang raced across his face, slashing at his eyes; the sands around him trembled, and then water smashed down on him, like falling mountain stones. He toppled over and one long wave swept over him, pulping into his bones and cracking open his skin. He sank further into the sands, and another wave fell out of the sky, and another wave; the water beat into his nostrils and his ears and his eyes. There was blood dropping from him before he could drag himself across the sands to the part of the pebble beaches where the water, the innocent smiling water, only lapped and trickled and seemed harmless as a child.

All his life since those days he had wanted to hide and run away from water, and always water had haunted him and mesmerised him and dominated his life. He wanted to flee from the mere sound and sight of it, yet he was irresistibly drawn to it. Still, on a moonlit evening like this, he would come walking over the fields and up to the silent, gleaming sheet of the reservoir. The water was cold and steely; even the occasional wink of light from the moon's caress of the flashing surface was a malevolent gleam, showing no sign of warmth. He thought, as he stood at one end of the parapet: The water has a stony face, and it rushes past relentlessly and endlessly. I stand here and a hundred thousand million drops of water sweep abreast of me and then are lost into the receding mysteries of night. I lose all sense of time and reality and there is nothing but the living, shining, sweeping water ... I see nothing, I hear nothing, I think of nothing but the huge, ceaseless wall of water. My heart grows cold and sinks inside me, daggers of fear prick my limbs and an icy hand caresses my spine. I am chained to this one spot on the bank, waiting in anguish for the water to rear into the air and fall upon me in some final deluge, drowning me and sweeping me away into some fathomless world of water.

And he would stand there, transfixed, until it really seemed to him that the water was moving, gathering together like a man's gigantic smashing fist. Then he might run and run and run along the bank, his feet crunching the mud, his coat flying, his mouth open and spittle flecking out of it, his eyes blind with terror – running like some hunted animal, until by some miracle the water stopped keeping pace with him, fell back, outrun and he scrambled down the steep sloping sides into the neighbouring lane.

It was as he stood in the lane that evening, breathless and trembling, smoothing down his coat and straightening his trousers, that he became aware, not for the first time, how his private, his unimaginable private world, had finally closed in on him. How all the exits were finally closed, how there was no lost hidden secret avenue of escape. How he was already imprisoned and marooned on some tiny islet of his own, surrounded by a sea of blind humanity which would some day rise up and engulf him.

The effect was to produce in him a strange, irrational exhilaration that sent him bounding along the lane, his limbs tingling, his heart suddenly pumping new excited blood, his mind filled with a whirl of images and memories and his lips forming into some tuneless but quite gay whistle. Had he stopped, or been able to rationalise, he might have remembered that in the face of great danger men often found this reserve of false exhilaration. But this was a thought which, consciously or unconsciously, he avoided, leaving him free to wander down the lane in these precious moments of unimagined secret vitality.

The only difference to mark that evening from other occasions was that when he came to the bend where the lane turned south his eye was caught by a glimmer of light coming from a copse running off the corner. Still with his jaunty walk, and imbued with a careless gaiety, he climbed down off the road and made his way in between the trees. As he did so the light grew brighter and bigger, and suddenly he realised it was the red glow of a fire.

Peering from behind a thick tree he found himself looking out on a tiny clearance in the copse. In the centre of this burned the fire, a huge affair of logs and branches and twigs. The flames leaped higher and higher, throwing off rainfalls of sparks, and lighting up the glade like some supernatural grotto. Behind the fire he saw the gleaming green and gold silhouette of a caravan – a gipsy caravan, one of the genuine old, smoky, dirty, slightly glamorous caravans, with chassis raised high in the air, tall grey wheels and painted emblems along the sides and around the front door. The door was open, and sitting on the steps were the gipsy and his wife; he an oldish man with thick grey hair and a scarf tucked high around his neck, she a woman with a bandana hiding her hair, and a thick brown coat huddled round her shoulders, her face wrinkled and lined. They were sitting on the top step looking' out on the fire and holding their hands up to the warmth. At the sight of them, almost opposite him, Raymond felt a pang of sympathy, remembering how he had sat at home in front of his fire. But oh, such a tiny and lonely fire; oh, such a lonely, lonely fire. And he felt next a spasm of jealousy to see the two of them there, side by side, warmth for each other.

And then, so eerily and unbelievable that for quite a time he wondered if he had sunk into some fairy-like dream, he became aware of a third person – a young gipsy girl. She seemed to float out of the darkness beyond the caravan, appearing suddenly like some woodland spirit in the full flaming glow of the fire. She was young, perhaps very young, but yet a woman, in the way of gipsies. She had long, raven-black hair that hung about her shoulders, tied across her head by a bright yellow handkerchief, whipped round in a knot at the back. The receded hair seemed to give a prominence to her face, so that it stood out in relief, a round, sensual whiteness, the lips opened wide to show a pure laugh of joy that had no relation to anything, yet was somehow part of her.

He supposed the girl had come from the back of the caravan, or perhaps had been gathering wood in the woods. Now she seemed inescapably part of the landscape, as if it were some ever-remembered painting – now, as she stood there thoughtfully, her head bent a little, her body curving towards the fire as if drawn despite itself by the warmth, one of her legs stretched forward slightly so that he caught the flash of brown and saw that her feet were bare.

The girl stood in that pose for several minutes, as if lost in some strange dream. As he watched, in his mood of exhilarated daring, he conceived the idea that in some way the girl was aware of him just as he was aware of her, that she was lost in the same dream as himself; that, while their bodies posed in scattered parts of that usually lonely wood, their spirits were soaring out into the night, converging and meeting in some secret place. So strong was the feeling that he gave himself up to it in entirety, feeling himself beside the girl, feeling her presence, her warmth, her breathtaking reality.

It was not until there was a stirring, and he saw the man climb down from the stairs and walk over towards where he was crouching that, unwillingly, he moved. With a last backward look, he tiptoed away, away from the warmth and the red flames, back into his personal darkness. And as he walked back, he felt the blood coursing in his veins, like some suddenly swollen river, and he thought: Was it a dream – oh, was it a dream? Was it some strange picture, some unbelievable memory, or was it there, a reality?

And the further he went into his lonely dreamlike darkness, the more he assured himself of the reality, of the fire and the flames, and of the dark, dark gipsy girl, standing poised like some goddess of the night. And then there arose a wild, uncontrollable singing in his heart, so that he cried out and went rushing back to the dark grey house possessed by his greatest madness of all, the dream that out of the night he had suddenly found a purpose and a light to his life.

VI

At nine o'clock on the Friday, Oliver and Raymond set off in the Lagonda for Bedruthan market. Frances was up early helping them to get ready, filling two thermoses full of coffee (Oliver always grumbled he could never get good coffee in restaurants) and standing guard over the barn doors when they and Mark were shepherding four startled nanny goats into the box trailer. For the children it was a weekly occasion of great excitement. They hurried through their breakfast in order to be able to slip down from the table and race round to the shed where the car and trailer were being manoeuvred into partnership.

'Ooh,' said Timothy disapprovingly. 'They're taking away Polly. Poor Polly.'

And he held a comforting hand out in the direction of Polly, who promptly lowered her white-flecked head and tried to butt Timothy and his hand.

'Careful, you little idiot!' exclaimed Oliver, panting. He and Raymond and Mark were each manhandling a goat into the container, and finding it hard work. The fourth goat stood to one side, its two beady brown eyes rolling round and round as if in nervous anticipation of its own fate to come. Goats represented a profitable side-line which Oliver had developed. They cost practically nothing to feed and he was able, by judiciously awaiting the right buyer, to sell them at a good profit.

Frances could not restrain a laugh as Oliver's goat twisted round and gave him a sharp prod in the rear, pushing him against the car bonnet.

'Ouch! Hey, mind, don't let her out!'

Expertly Frances caught at the halter, pulled the bucking goat back and handed her to Oliver. She was fond of goats. She remembered with affection a short period in the early years where they had for a time practically lived on goats – goats' milk for drink, and a lucky sale of three good breeders for money.

'Good luck with the sales. No cut-price!' she called out as at last they bolted the trailer.

'What do you take me for?' said Oliver over his shoulder as he climbed into the driving seat. 'I'm known all over Cornwall as the man with a stone for a heart.'

He leaned out of the window, grinning at her with sudden affection.

'Goodbye, darling. Look after the two horrors.'

'Goodbye,' said Frances. 'Goodbye. Take care of yourselves.'

She felt her cheeks flush as an inexplicable wave of tenderness flooded over her, so that she felt impelled to put one hand on the car window beside Oliver. Seeing him as he was then, the bulky leather coat buttoned up to his neck and the old white and blue scarf wound high, the bright look of excitement enlivening his eyes, she was aware how deep and solid was her love for him.

'Goodbye, you awful children,' called Oliver, leaning further over the side.

'Goodbye, Daddy.'

They clambered on to the running-board.

'Can we ride to the gate?'

'Well, all right. Theresa, you go to Raymond's side. Are you right, Raymond?'

Raymond was right, tucked well in. He leaned over and put a guarding arm under Theresa's waist, as she clung on to the running-board. Timothy, the other side, looked superior. He did not need a guarding arm.

With a jerk and a high-pitched roar the Lagonda started, trundled over the rough mud of the yard and down the short lane to the white gate, the trailer and its round-eyed contents bobbing about nervously in the wake. As it stopped the two temporary passengers ran and swung open the gate. Then the cargo was off again – this time gathering speed steadily until it topped the rise leading to the main road.

Frances waited, immobile, as the children raced each other back to her, helter-skelter, hair flying and cheeks red with puffing.

'I won, I won!' cried Timothy, clutching at her outstretched hand.

'Only because you cheated. You pushed.'

'I didn't cheat – did, I Mummy?'

'I expect you did, darling. Let's call it a dead heat, shall we?'

She was conscious of Mark standing behind her, watching the car until it was lost to view. He turned to her with a smile.

'An exciting beginning.'

'Yes.'

He grinned down at the children. He liked children; he had always got on well with them.

'Hullo, Mark. Will you play with us?'

'Well, I'm afraid not. There is work to do, you know. You can help with the milking tonight, if you like.'

Mark looked across at Frances and made as if to speak. She shook her head and slanted her eyes at the children. He nodded, imperceptibly.

'I'll just see to the horses,' he said. He paused. 'After that I'm going out to the potato field. I'll be there all morning.'

She knew, without looking at him, that the words were an invitation, and despite herself she felt a shiver of impending happiness run through her.

'Very well,' she said coolly. Then, turning: 'Come on, children. Let's go and see what Edith is doing.'

She took them, one by each hand, and they walked slowly across the yard, and through the white stone porchway into the house.

Watching them go Mark felt a sense of peace and satisfaction, a curious impersonal pleasure so that he almost would have liked to see Oliver walking at the other side. Which was an odd thought, indeed, he thought wryly, for a man whose morning and life was made sunny and alive only at the thoughts of seeing her, of holding her in his arms.

He turned and went towards the cowshed, and Frances heard him whistling a gay, dancing tune, until he closed the door behind him.

Inside, she let the children go ahead of her into the ktichen while she stood at the door of the library. She was remembering that time some weeks ago when she had identified each room of the house with one of its inhabitants. The library with Raymond. ... And now, in a few days, it had become Mark's room, too. She was remembering that evening two days ago, and how they had just sat there for an hour in each other's arms, watching the sun until it had quite disappeared and at last they heard the sound of Oliver and the children from across the field. It had not been like any other love-making she had known; there had not been the urgency that she expected – that, possibly, he expected. It was rather as if, in coming together, both had been fused into the same pool of quietude and peace. So that, without any premeditation, they had been content to sit and touch each other and exchange long, gentle kisses, looking into each other's eyes with the wondering, caressing look of a love discovered. The hour had gone like a stolen moment; and yet the moment in memory was a deepening pool whose intensity remained unsuspected, and perhaps immeasurable.

The next day she had seen him only to talk to out of the kitchen window. He had leaned there with the sun catching his straw-scattered hair and she had seen him as he really was, as someone warm and human, and burning with a creative fire, as someone intimate and under her skin, and she had felt the reality of her love towards him.

She had told the others about his piano playing. That evening after an early supper, Mark had been invited in, and had played the piano while she and Oliver and Raymond sat around the warm red glow of the stove in the library. They had put out the light, and left the room in the subdued rosy glow of the fire, with two candles flickering above the piano. Mark had played from memory, melodies that streamed back into his mind and his fingers, each one seeming to unloosen another

chord, another prison strait-jacket, so that his fingers leaped
and danced and jigged – so that, in the end, out of sheer
flamboyant happiness, he played a piece of Ravel's *Daphnis and
Chloë* suite that had been the last thing he practised for a concert
at Hamburg which he never gave. It was music which he felt to
be on the surface rather than deep down, but which captured
in vivid flashes some ecstatic descriptive passages of daybreak
and dusk, to the world of nature awakening. As he played he
seemed to give it a new beauty, almost a wistfulness – or at least
so it seemed to her, knowing what he felt, knowing the joy and
the awakening that was growing in him, and so became
expressed in his playing.

Mark played for an hour while they sat in silence, wrapped
in the music and their thoughts. Watching under half-closed
eyes Frances saw Oliver nodding quietly but knew that he was
not asleep – knew that in his own way he was captured and
enriched by it. And then, turning, she watched Raymond, and
could almost read on his darkened, half-averted face, the
gamut of his strange uneasy mind; how he hated her asking
Mark to come at all, how he sat there entrenched in walls of
resentment yet unable, despite himself, to resist the almost
inhuman beauty which somehow Mark had produced out of
the old, not very well tuned piano. For there could be no
mistake about it: in Mark's possession lay the genius of an
immortal pianist.

'My God, Mark, you're wasting your time on a farm,' said
Oliver gruffly, when it was over. 'Here, have a drink on it.'

'You played beautifully. Thank you,' said Frances.

Mark hesitated, conscious suddenly of his exhaustion after
the long period of playing. But he took the proffered drink
with a faint smile, held the glass politely towards Oliver and
Frances, and drank.

Then, seeing Raymond still slouched in his chair, staring
fixedly into the centre of the stove's red glow, Mark's smile
vanished and Frances saw the look of hurt shadowing his face.

'I think I will go now,' he said quickly. 'Thank you so much.
It was – a great deal to me – to be allowed to play.'

'You must play again another evening,' said Oliver.

Mark nodded. Then, with a gentle smile at Frances, he went through the door.

'A bit startling, wasn't he?' Oliver frowned. 'What a waste. I wonder if we can do anything about it? He could play at a village concert, for a start.'

'He plays superbly,' said Frances. She walked slowly to the back of Raymond's chair, and put her hands on the two tall burnished tops. Oh, Raymond, she thought, don't do this, don't turn in further and further, like some toenail that must bury itself forever into its own flesh – please, Raymond, for my sake emerge, burst the bonds of this bitterness, look at the sun instead of just lifeless fire. Don't let the hate and the bitterness overwhelm you, becoming you. Don't …

She bit her lip.

'Didn't you enjoy it, Raymond?'

He stirred, uneasily, unhappily.

'Yes … Of course. It was very clever.' He laughed metallically. There, he had said the words, he had made the pretence. 'Wish I could play as well.'

Awkwardly, he put one arm up and touched his sister's hand. Poor Frances. He always disappointed her. He could never quite become what she had wanted him to be. He sighed; said nothing; stared again into the flames.

And she sighed, too, and turned away. Raymond, Raymond – who was, she realised, so like Mark whom he hated. Suddenly she saw, pinpointed in her own life, the last possible solution for Raymond, the one that if only she had not been his sister it might have been within her power to provide. Instead she would always fail in her attempts to comfort and sustain him. The pattern became unbearable: for only some great love could make him whole, and yet his disintegration must separate him forever from such a love.

How, hearing the children calling to her from the kitchen, she turned away from the library and it secret memories, went across the silent hallway and into the kitchen.

'What is it now?'

'Mummy, look what Edith's brought us. An apple cake!'

Edith's husband was the village baker, a fact responsible for a whole series of tasty 'extras' making their appearance on the menu at the farm.

'You can have a piece, Mummy.'

'Well … thanks. That's very considerate of you.'

Timothy approached the cake in a proprietary manner, holding the carving knife rather as if it were a magic wand. His small, pert face was at once screwed up in an intense frown of concentration, his eyes narrowed, his lower lip bitten inwards. Watching, she saw about him a dozen little things that reminded her forcibly of Oliver: the concentration, the determination, even the slight air of arrogance. He was Oliver's boy, he would make his mark one way or another. She smiled. Well, that was how it should be, the son to the father, the daughter to the mother – that was fair enough. For Theresa was equally her mother's reflection. Often she would sit at the window, watching the two of them play, hunting invaders or building houses, concocting a wild variety of fantasy games, and she would have the eerie sensation that she was watching herself in some magic mirror that looked back down the years – that it was she and not Theresa dancing among the grass, long pigtails flying and pretty red bow catching in the overhanging tree branches. Except that she had never had quite the same pronounced element of beauty. Theresa was going to grow up into a beautiful woman, of that she felt sure. And, she hoped, a wise one as well. What would become of her? Or Timothy? Would he become another farmer? Or would he become a business man, or something unforeseen, a sailor perhaps? Whatever it was he would become a someone at it … And Theresa? What would you like to be when you grow up, darling?

Almost as if in reply to her unspoken question, the little girl with the dark serious face executed a graceful pirouette around the kitchen table, all the while making rude faces at Timothy.

'Hurry up, for goodness sake, slow-coach. Mummy and I are hungry.'

Yes, she had thought it before; Theresa would become a dancer, or perhaps an actress. She would be, in some ways, more of a person and an individual than her mother. For

Theresa there would be the chance to achieve those extra ambitions that had always slumbered, could now never be resurrected, in Frances.

And yet, she thought, taking the rich piece of apple cake which Timothy presented to her with a flourish, yet I could not have had them *and* what else I have had – oh, and yet, I would not want you, Theresa, to be just a dancer, to become just a figurehead, a mime, a piece of scenery – oh, my dear, I want you to have love and marriage and a home as well. It is just that for some women I feel there can be both, and there is something about you that makes me feel you are one of those women.

She bit at her cake, almost angrily, as the confusion of thoughts raged through her, as the quicksand nature of her position struck her. Supposing some day she wanted to tell Theresa about herself, about Mark. Could she make her understand? Could she make anyone – Oliver – understand? *Was* it explainable?

She moved over to the sink, picked up a dish cloth and began drying the plates and cups which Edith was lathering and heaping up. She rubbed round the edge of one of the plates, following the neat yet intricate floral pattern like a pathway through a maze.

Did she understand it herself? A week ago, even, she would have laughed at the idea of herself turning to a lover. It was one of those ideas which a comfortably married couple talk or dream about, usually as a joke, sometimes perhaps with a vague wistfulness – seldom with any predetermination. It was an idea, surely, which was only put into practice by the unhappy, the misfits?

Oh, but we are not these, Oliver dearest, she thought, and her hand stopped at one point on the plate and pressed into its hard, unrevealing surface. Or are we, she thought, with a detachment that surprised her. And when, despite this, there was a rush of tenderness to her heart she was glad, glad to have reassurance for what she had always known deep down. There was too much solidity and worth, too much built out of love, in those ten years for it to be nullified or squandered, reduced in any way.

She and Oliver, the children, the home, their whole life,

formed a pattern. She saw that now clearly, as clearly as, looking out of the kitchen window, she saw the familiar yard, the familiar coal dump, beyond it the familiar fields rolling into oblivion – it was a pattern of the past and the future.

But there was also the present. She put down the plate and went over to the door, staring out across the fields. Would she ever be able to explain that? She supposed, never. And yet, she was conscious with some slight surprise, she could not feel, could not pretend to feel, any sense of guilt. Because, and she knew this with the inexplicable sureness of a woman, there was nothing to be guilty about. She knew that her love for Oliver was as real and unharmed as ever – indeed, what had become doubtful recently was Oliver's love for her. It was besides and apart from this love that she felt upon her this sudden sweet, rather gentle drawing towards Mark – something that had welled up simultaneously between them as if created out of the very nothingness that had laid between them: a private intimate thing, secret to them, lost without them, harmless beyond their closed circle ...

She sighed, knowing that no matter what she thought, no matter how she saw the whole, the meaning and the value, there was no guarantee of harmlessness. For she would be blind to ignore the possible, indeed the probable – would it not perhaps harm everything? And therefore would not the conventional, even the sensible, procedure be to stop now, to make an end while there was time – while, with the surgeon's cruelty, a swift oblivion might be achieved that would later perhaps be impossible? It was possible. It lay in her hands. She could withdraw, become remote. Or Mark could be transferred somewhere else. But at the thought she felt a constriction at her heart, felt an ache of pain as she saw his face mirroring in its shadows all the years of his loneliness and impotence, the hands frozen and the tongue halted, a world at a standstill.

She remembered the night they had come together in the red glow of a dying sun, and how suddenly it seemed as if out of the dead sun he was rising, a new sun – how in the very moment of their first kiss it was as if, in her blind urge towards him, she had found the only key to unlock the walls of bitter armour that had grown around him, that soon would have rusted and died with all that was contained. Oh, it would have been a denial of her own self to turn now, to pretend that which did not exist, to deny that there was a love between them, that there was something flowing in and out of them like fresh water. Theresa, one day you would understand. But Timothy, and Oliver – Oliver, would you ever understand?

And at the anguish of the thought she was forced to lean against the door and drop her head downwards, so that Edith came across, anxiously.

'Are you all right, Mrs Williams? Feeling faint?'

She shook herself, straightened.

'No – no, it's all right, Edith. Quite all right.'

And suddenly, she *was* all right. Suddenly she had a sense of the inevitability of events, and the futility of prognostication. It was not that she had made any headway through the jungle, nor come to any decision. It was simply that she realised that in some way the decision had made itself and that she was now a part of a process – that the ultimate was irresistible, save that somehow it was limited in time.

'Quite all right, thank you, Edith,' she said, and there was an uplift in her voice that convinced Edith that she must have been mistaken.

And now she was aware of no regrets towards Oliver, racing through the hot day and dusty roads, because she felt towards him only the truth of their love, and for that there need be no regrets. Now she was emptied of all shadows and torturous arguments and opened to the glorious warmth and delight of all lovers – now she thought only, with a great urgency, about Mark, somewhere far out across the fields, stooping over the long lines of potatoes, sweating perhaps, brown from the sun, his hair tumbling forwards, his body aching and tensed, awaiting her cool touch as she awaited his warm one, both of them awaiting a release and a renewal.

She teased Timothy gaily to give her another piece of apple cake, and crunched it hungrily between her teeth. In all the rush and bother she had forgotten to have any breakfast herself. She looked at the clock.

'Heavens, it's eleven o'clock.'

Outside she was conscious of the sun rising higher and higher, like a benevolent waiting orb. And the sky blue all around it, like the sea.

'Now, children, what about doing some gardening? When did you last look at your garden, either of you?'

They muttered, grudgingly, that it had been quite a time.

'Well, don't you think it's time you gave it just a little attention? I'll tell you what, you weed and rake it out, both of you, and then when you come in Edith will give you a nice hot lunch, eh?'

They looked at each other. Momentarily she envied their world, so factual and simple, so uninhibited.

'Oh, all right. Bags I the spade first!'

And when Theresa pouted, Timothy explained righteously.

'It's quite fair. I have the spade and you have the fork, then I have the fork and you have the spade. Then we'll both rake.'

'Silly,' said Theresa pityingly, as they scampered out of doors in search of the all-important tools. 'How can we both rake when we have a separate garden each? And mine's ever so much better than yours. I'll bet you haven't —'

Frances listened laughingly until a turn in the corridor walls cut off the familiar voices as finally as an axe. She turned to Edith.

'I think I'll leave things to you, now. Give them some of the lamb for lunch — and see that Timmy eats all his. I — I think I'll go for a walk. It's such a fine day I can't resist it any longer.'

'That's right, Mrs Williams.' Edith nodded wisely, with the condescension of all village folk who never walk a foot for pleasure because they spend such a time walking for work. 'You have a nice walk and I'll see to things.'

Frances nodded absent-mindedly, and went towards the door.

'Are you going out like that?'

'What?'

She saw Edith looking surprised, saw that she was still wearing the dirty overall.

'Oh, I hadn't noticed. No, of course not. What a wreck I look!'

And suddenly she was giggling like a schoolgirl, running upstairs and thinking, good heavens, is that all I care? Don't I want to please him, don't I want to make myself look beautiful so that he will love me all the more? And as she went into the bedroom and began throwing off her things, she knew somehow that she was going to look beautiful.

*

Mark saw her coming across the field as he was bent down between the straight lines of potato plants, and at the sight of her he felt transfixed, unable or unwilling to move, wanting only for ever and ever to be watching this woman in the blue costume floating across the edge of the field like the colourful figurehead of some ship. He was reminded of a figurehead he used to see on a Swedish ship in Hamburg docks – one of those strong Nordic women's faces with the long flaxen hair that flowed out behind, enveloping their body from view. Only that had been wooden and static – she was pliable, warm flesh and blood; she seemed, momentarily, to be at one with the sun and the wind and the whole swaying panorama of the country afternoon.

He marvelled yet again at the fantasy world through which he had achieved this, how just when he had felt himself at the end of all life, beyond further struggling, about to submerge into a morass of hopelessness, she had turned towards him, like – like a sun, a new sun. In his hands, even as the thoughts formed in his mind, he felt the itch of excitement, thinking: I could compose music like that, I could create something worthy of her, in honour of a new sun – I can, and someday I will. Great music.

For you, Frances, he thought, watching her coming nearer and nearer, surrounded by a faint shimmer of heat, and wondering if perhaps she was not a mirage of the mid-day sun – knowing that in an ultimate sense she was.

She did not see his bent figure, hidden among the green sea, until she was almost abreast. He stood up suddenly, like a tree shooting out of the ground.

'Oh!' she cried, raising a hand and then, recognising him, as suddenly dropping it. She smiled across the remaining rows of plants. 'Mark. Mark ...'

'Frances!' He jumped across the rows, one, two, three, his hands reaching out to meet hers. 'At last! All the morning I have been waiting, so impatiently. Every time I bent down once, so also I looked once to the horizon. And now at last you have come.'

He looked down at his hands.

'They are so dirty. I –'

'No, please, I like them – love them – as they are.'

She said the words softly, a little shyly, and it made him love her that moment with an unbearable tension. Slowly she cupped his hands together and raised them and pressed them against her cheek.

'There is so much, perhaps all of you in your hands, Mark. I can feel it now, all the pride and the hope and the loneliness and the suffering, I can feel it here against my cheek,'

'And I,' he whispered. 'I can feel, against your cheek, such warmth and love that I would never want to move my hands, unless it were to touch your other cheek.'

They stood together for a moment and then she moved away, trembling slightly. Already, as if part of a predestined dream, she could feel the world outside them disappearing, lost behind some enormous blue sky that now was gradually closing in upon them.

'I brought some sandwiches,' she said. 'I thought we would go and have a little picnic somewhere.'

'Yes, Frances. That would be nice. Our first picnic ...'

Almost roughly, he pulled her to him and kissed her. Feeling his lips upon hers, so slack and open with desire, she felt his tremendous urgency communicated to her. The blood raced through her veins and she returned his kiss for a moment before, gently, she freed herself.

'Not here, Mark.'

He smiled at her, a long slow smile from which she could never have escaped.

'*Liebestraum,*' he said.

'What's that?'

'It means, my dream of love – or as you English would say, perhaps, my darling.'

'*Liebestraum.*' She repeated the word awkwardly, and then again, savouring it on her tongue tip. '*Liebestraum.* It's a lovely word.'

'And warm, Frances. Like you.'

He took her arm, winding his fingers around under the elbow.

'Let us go to our picnic. There is a haystack at the end of the field. The sun has dried it through – it is wonderfully comfortable. I often sit there and have my lunch. I feel like a king, with a huge bed of my own. But –'

He glanced down at her puckered, serious face, with a quirk of amusement.

'I will tell you a secret.'

'What?'

'– sometimes the king longed for a queen. He was so lonely.'

They walked along slowly, in swinging movement, their bodies gently touching.

'I was so proud of you last night,' she said. 'You played wonderfully.'

'I played for you.'

'And you were happy – to be playing again?'

His grip tightened.

'Happier than you can imagine. Oh yes, despite your brother's frowns, despite anything, I felt a wonderful vitality. I could have played for hours and hours.'

'Oh, I wish you had!'

'Perhaps for days and days. Oh, Frances beloved, you have no idea – I cannot begin to tell you – do you know what you are doing?'

His tone dropped into a whisper.

'You are giving me life, when you give me love.'

She pressed his hand gently.

And now they were in sight of the tumbled haystack, nestling in a corner, burnt brown gold in the mid-day sun, seeming to lie before them like yet another sun. Suddenly it seemed that there was no further need for conversation, for there was nothing further to say.

They walked slowly, dreamily, towards the haystack, and with each step they took it seemed to her that this great blue dome of eternity was closing around them closer and closer, until they were alone, absolutely alone, in a world that was their own.

And as this knowledge enveloped her with its certainty she felt the weight of everything else vanishing, felt herself delicately stripped of the whole clutter of her everyday life so that she was now at peace with herself, able to be herself.

And being herself she knew only the great sun burning down upon them coursing into her veins and limbs, knew only the great fire burning up within her, knew only the warmth of Mark beside her, the burning warmth of him and the great sea of love into which they sank with each step so that almost unconsciously his arms were around her, touching her gently on the curve of her shoulder, on the nape of her neck, half carrying her, half lifting her – until with simplicity and happiness she raised her own hands and slipped them swiftly, almost greedily, around Mark's neck, entwining them with finality, and whispered, 'Love me, for I love you, *Liebestraum*.'

The haystack was a bed of gold, warm and bubbling with laughter and life, and they sank into it like children, and as innocently, bringing to each other the purity and the sweet renewal of their love, bringing to each other a drop more of wonderment and a drop more of marvel in the mysterious sea of their existence.

*

Raymond sat in the Antelope Hotel bar while Oliver disposed of the goats. The town was crowded with farmers and motor cars, great lorry loads of cattle, a bustle of country people about the streets – the smell of farmyards transported into the old market square. At one time he would have found the scene exciting and colourful; he might even, in his more purposeful days, have jotted little notes in his diary, flashes of description about the dour farmers and their wives, the red-faced auctioneers, the sweating market-assistants – even about some of the animals, the way one shy, valuable colt neighed and looked about like one lost in a madman's foundry.

All that was gone, he knew, sitting there and sipping at his beer. Gin would have been more to his preference, but now, to such a pass was his life, he could hardly afford gin. He sat at a small table in the corner of the oak-beamed room, his back tucked between a join in two walls so that he was in some subtle way cut off from the rest of the room, a spectator but not a companion of the group of farmers arguing about prices at the bar, of the two army lieutenants sitting in the far corner, of the party, perhaps a marriage party, of men and women occupying the centre of the room.

He was, already, cut off. The knowledge impinged upon him daily, in some way came as a relief. With each day that he accepted it so he was freed of the necessity of making any decisions. There were no more to be made; they had been made, forever.

Sometimes he repeated the thought over and over to himself, parrot-like. The decisions have been made. The words took on a dry, macabre sound, like a line of T.S. Eliot's, perhaps more like a legal phrase, a judge's summing up. With the black cap on, he thought, and smiled ironically, and raised his glass.

But with the glass still at his mouth, looking down so that he peered deep into the heart of the brown liquid world, he searched secretly for that flicker of hope that had come to him the other night. In the brown mirror of his glass he saw, like cinematic flashbacks, the strange new mystery of his life that emerged at night-time, when the friendly darkness brought safety from the brittle blaze and revelation of daytime.

The very night after his discovery of the gipsy encampment he had crept down again by the silent reservoir, treading softly so that no one and nothing in the world should be aware of his presence, finding his way almost by instinct – for there was hardly any light showing that evening – to the tiny wood and the caravan. He lay there, half buried in dead leaves, against the hard skin of an oak tree, watching ... seeing the old gipsy staring morosely and silently, occasionally poking at the small fire, while his wife again sat on the step and knitted and flicked with her long needles.

At last the old couple disappeared, leaving the young raven-haired gypsy girl, curled up in the contemplative silence, staring deep into the flames. He lay there for what seemed hours and hours, while the fire flickered lower and the young girl sat there silent and unmoving, and gradually his imagination grew up into the great darkness of the night and he saw himself stepping like some ghost out of the embers, like some newly risen figure, a strange dark tall man with a flashing sword ... At his appearance the girl seemed to spring into life, her face lit up and her arms leapt to embrace him. At his bidding she began dancing, at first slowly, her thick limbs glinting with a strange ethereal whiteness, softly outlined against the red firelight.

Then, as his sword slashed through the air in an angry command, the girl whirled round, and transfixed into a marble statue, offered up her gleaming face, her glaring eyes, her curved straining body, her firm rounded breasts; her swaying hands outstretched in a queer gesture of pleading and surrender. And then it seemed that the girl became possessed of some subtle rhythm imposed from within. She began writhing and twisting in a weird dance, moving round and round the fire, always keeping her eyes fixed on him. Soon her body and face and arms were bathed in sweat, but still she danced on. It was as if some ghostly music rose to a crescendo, and the girl's limbs whirred and hissed frantically through the air in an effort to keep pace ... and all at once the sounds vanished, the dance stopped, all at once the girl poised in a beautiful gesture of surrender and he strode towards her taking her in his arms, melting into the warmth of her flesh ...

He could hardly believe, when at last the girl stood up and sighed and went into the caravan, that she had indeed sat there all the evening like some contemplative Buddha, that she had not indeed been whirling around and awaiting him.

The next night he came again, and the night after, and each time as he set out across the dark lonely fields he convinced himself that what happened was not a dream, would no longer be a dream, each time he convinced himself that there was some subterranean bond already established between himself and the girl – that even that night, though he did not move from his hiding-place, though the girl stared deep and mysteriously into the fire, yet their minds were meeting somewhere out in the dark night, yet their bodies were together and there was a fusion between them, even though all the night and the fire and the impenetrability of withdrawn humanity lay between them.

And I shall be there again tonight, he knew, draining the last long brown blob of liquid, and I shall be there again tomorrow night, he thought, hating himself and it all, hating even the taste of the beer that was no longer beer, plonking down the glass with a heavy final motion. Gazing round the room as at some other world, a museum beyond his conception.

'Hullo,' said a familiar voice, and he saw Oliver standing at his side. Oliver's thick grey tweed and bulging pockets, Oliver with a drink in one hand and a pipe in the other; comforting Oliver.

'Have a drink?'

'No, thanks, Oliver. Had enough.'

'Good ... I was wondering if you'd mind if we started back?'

'Why – no.' And suddenly, because rendered more sensitive by his own unhappiness, he looked up swiftly and into Oliver's eyes, and saw behind their bland inquiry a host of flecking shadows such as raced across his own world. Only he thought, self-pityingly, there have been shadows in my world, I suppose, since I was born – certainly since school, certainly since the business, certainly since the *war* – and there he closed his mind.

But a great human pity for Oliver suddenly welled up in him, though he knew not why.

'Of course, Oliver. What about lunch though? It's a long drive.'

Oliver drained his glass quickly.

'We can have something when we get back.'

'Suits me.'

Oliver knocked his pipe out against the mantelpiece. He had only just lit it, Raymond remembered.

'Shall we go?'

He walked out a little way behind Oliver, threading a way through the strangers, clinging in his mind to the one familiar being, the square straight back ahead of him. He wished he had Oliver's decisiveness, Oliver's purpose, Oliver's ability. Or did he? Did he really wish to be anyone else? No, he thought, surprisedly, not really. And in the false momentary glow of this deception he felt again a worry and a sadness for Oliver, who was not himself, striding ahead of him across the cobbled pavement to the waiting Lagonda, the mud-spattered green monster of the farm.

He got in, snuggled down behind the windscreen, put a rug around his feet and tucked away all the draught. The hood was down, there would be a deuce of a wind as they roared up and down the bleak hilly parts. He grinned, imbued with a surge of Oliver's own exhilaration.

'All right, Oliver. Let her rip. Let her fly through the air. Let's go!'

And in a few moments, it seemed, they were through the long town road and out – out into an undulating world of fields and lonely copses and occasional blobs of dark woods, a world slashed across with the single silver-shining arterial road.

'Here we go then!' Oliver shouted back, before the wind ripped the words away into wasteland.

And he crouched low over the wheel and held on to it with the half-tense, half-light grip of the experienced motorist, hung on to it like his own life, while his foot pressed remorselessly down on the accelerator pedal, while he watched the road ahead, every now and then glancing with swift nervous movements at the needle, watching it creep up and up, watching it surge and surge, feeling the wind howling, the air blasting, the trees and the fields and the sky coming to meet them, knowing nothing about them except that they must come and go quickly, because for some reason he could not know about he wanted to be home, he wanted to return to that place where his roots where, he wanted to kill and destroy this restless aching sense of unease that had haunted him lately, that now seemed to be with him daily, that today had fallen upon him like a cloud that he could not pierce or splinter, could not push aside.

And as the thick rubber wheels of the Lagonda pounded and hissed across the dry roads, slithering around long corners, racing up and down the smooth hills, they seemed to whistle out some underground refrain that he could just feel through the vibrating of the wheel, and to which he matched his thoughts and whispered over and over again within himself: I want to go home, I want to go home, I want to go home. He was amazed and at once ashamed, but also a little frightened, at finding himself a boy and a child again, sitting there alone and lost, and crying for the security and the foundation of his life, possessed only by the one desire that he should reach it before – before – before –? Before what, he wondered, as he kept his head bent low behind the windscreen and watched the flecks of dust and dirt and insects hammered against it and then blown off like the dry dust of men's shoes – before what?

And that he could not imagine, except that he knew now, already, in his heart, that it was too late, that driving a motor car at breakneck speed was no longer anything more than a subterfuge, a false god.

*

An hour later, as the Lagonda swung over the crest of the lane and down into the farmyard, they saw Frances and Mark coming from the long green potato field, holding hands like any sunny afternoon lovers.

VII

The piano was playing softly as Raymond came down the stairs from his attic. Behind him lay the torn-up scraps of paper, the open but deserted typewriter, the heap of paper clips he had twisted into unrecognisable shapes between his fingers. He was in a mood for harsh, discordant music, for rude chords that shattered the early evening stillness and vibrated on afterwards in the mind and body; not for a rippling river of peace and gentle whispering.

He stood still at the top of the main stairway, one hand on the mahogany banister, frowning, trying to will the music to stop. Oh, if it was his house there would be no sound of that music now, there would be either an absolute silence or a raging of winds and the hollow thump of thunder, anything but this intrusive, quiet echo. And he thought with inner excitement of such a house that was his alone, of barricading all the doors and windows and striding about the corridors and up and down great staircases, opening and shutting doors; of being alone with this house to do with as he willed – a house where the storms and the upheavals were great Wagnerian affairs, tempestuous and elemental. Not quiet and subtle, not persuasive and unavoidable, like the theme of the piano music, like the fact of the piano player and Frances.

Curse it! At least he was a part of the house, an echo in the attic, at least he belonged there as much as a room and a place at the dining-table – more so than Mark, sitting at the piano, evening after evening. Why should there be this music intruding from outside? And he thought indignantly of the quietude of the library, the long solemn rows of books, the corner where you could sit and read while the sun poured through the French windows – now all lost to him, because of the sound of a piano.

He went swiftly down the stairs, treading each footstep firmly and squarely into the soft red carpet, feeling himself embarked on some procedure more definite and purposeful than usual. He entered the library noisily, without knocking, and stood just inside the door.

Mark was playing, his tall form bent over the piano, absorbed in the gentle intricacies of a Chopin nocturne. There was a sheet of music open now before him; already he was able to widen and strengthen his technique, already he felt himself recovering his urge for exploration and development.

He did not turn round when Raymond entered but went on playing, nodding his head occasionally as if entirely absorbed by the music.

Raymond stood for a while, his eyes burning into the crouched back, then walked over to the bookshelves. He was breathing heavily, his face flushed, his being ultra-conscious of Mark sitting there, a few feet away, wrapped in some satisfying world to which he had no access.

He picked out a book, fingering the red leather backing; *Wuthering Heights* by Emily Brontë; looking at the gold printed title without emotion, thinking to himself mechanically, I have read this before. He ran his fingers further along; *The Tenant of Wildfell Hall* by Anne Brontë; that, too, he had read and re-read. Perhaps there was no book there that he hadn't read before, those long silent hours of the night, under the little silver lamp? He found that only one part of his mind was thinking and asking these irrelevant, mechanical questions. The rest, the human part of his mind, was thinking with venom about Mark, sitting there, the brown-jacket intruder into the life of the house, of Oliver, of himself – of Frances. The brown intruder, the brown German intruder, whom, he realised suddenly, he hated.

The music stopped, whether at the end of the piece or in the middle he never was quite sure. Mark shrugged his shoulders, without turning round.

'I am sorry if my playing had disturbed you. I will go now.'

He met Raymond's gaze for a moment and then looked away, a movement of pain crossing his face. He began to collect the music together.

Raymond stood there with the book of Anne Brontë's still in his hands, now opened, though he saw not a word on the page – his eyes still looking at Mark, and yet beyond him. He was conscious that normally he would have said, politely: Please do go on playing – would have been, at the least, civil. Instead he was afraid to speak for fear of what hasty words might tumble off his tongue.

'You do not like me. You would rather I was not here.' Mark spoke quietly. 'I am aware of that. It would be difficult for me not to be.' He shrugged. 'I wish it were not so, but if it is – then it cannot be helped. I only think to myself, what a pity, when we are two such unconnected people, when we have no reason to come together either in conflict or in pleasure ... A waste of energy, that is what I was thinking.'

'I'm not interested in what you think.' Raymond's face was now a dark red. His fingers tightened round the book. 'I certainly share your view that we are unconnected. I can think of no more unpleasant connection. I only wish you were entirely unconnected not only with me, but this whole place. I wish –'

His voice trailed off and he moved the book helplessly from one hand to the other, as if trying to find a responsible authority to accept not only the book, but his unspoken wish.

'You wish I would go away?'

Mark sighed, and got up, holding the music sheets under his arm. He turned for a moment to look out of the window, wondering if there might be a sun there again, a flicker of gold hope. But the sky was grey and dusk covered.

'I don't know why it should cause me such sadness, such pain even – that you should resent me so much,' he said slowly.

Raymond's lips twisted.

'No doubt you would wish to be on as friendly terms with the rest of Frances' – Mrs Williams' – family as you are with her. Isn't that a simple enough reason? – if you must have one to satisfy your tortured conscience!'

It pleased him to see Mark's face turn pale, to see the tremble of the lower lip and know that the sneer had wounded. And yet, even as he felt the almost sadistic pleasure of seeing his words give pain he was somehow unprepared to see the sparkle of tears welling up in Mark's eyes – tears that he dammed up by an effort of angry pride, but which were there like the rain gathered within a dusky cloud. He had so often fought against tears himself, he knew so well the depth of feeling that must lie behind, that he could not resist being touched – could not help a murmur of sympathy travelling through his mind and into silent echoes.

And yet, even as he felt this strange sympathy and understanding, some other nagging emotion prodded more words out of him.

'Well? Isn't that so?'

Mark stood quite still, looking away, his hands clenching and unclenching. Then, without another word, he turned and walked swiftly across the library, his wooden soles echoing like drumbeats on the polished wood floor. Over to the door and, in an instance, out into oblivion.

Raymond watched him go carefully, his eyes following every movement, his ears checking the regular click-click of the boots. But when he was alone in the library and looked at the piano, still open, he was conscious of an uneasy sense of guilt. God, there was so much misery in the world – he felt ashamed that he might have intruded his hate upon some tiny oasis of happiness.

He was uneasy and on the defensive, therefore, when Frances came in quietly and said:

'I thought Mark would be practising.'

'He's gone.'

'Oh!' She looked puzzled. 'It's very early for him to finish. He usually plays for an hour at least.'

'I – he's gone, I tell you.'

She came over to him slowly, her eyes steady on him. He looked away, at the bookshelves.

'I've been looking up – some of the Brontë books,' he said hastily.

'Have you? Raymond, what made Mark go so early?'

'I don't know – perhaps because he didn't like my company.'

'Or could it be that you didn't like his?'

Raymond flushed.

'It's true I don't like it much. There's nothing wrong in that, is there?'

Frances sighed. She turned away and sat herself at the table.

'No. No, we can't be what we're not, we can't feel what we don't feel, I suppose. All the same, I do wish ...'

Despite himself, Raymond gave a sardonic laugh.

'Well, I must say that's a joke. First one wants me to be friendly, now the other –'

Frances looked up sharply.

'What do you mean by that?'

He looked down at her face, now stern, but usually so soft and lovely – often of late, he had noticed, alight with what he could only suppose was the glow of being in love, of feeling love. Was it wrong, then, he wondered, was anything wrong that gave people a warm glow, that lit up their lives, that brought new life to them? Suddenly aware of the ache of his whole being for just that experience, he softened towards his sister.

'Oh, Frances!' He came and stood behind her and put his hand in her thick unruly hair, spreading it outwards over her shoulders.

'Oh, Frances, I want you to be happy.'

'That's very considerate of you.' At once she was sorry for the impetuous sarcasm. She put her hand up quickly to touch his. 'No, that's silly of me, trying to be sarcastic. You're much better at it than me!'

'How right you are – oh, I don't want to hurt you, Frances, I don't want to intrude. Why should I?' He nearly said, I'm only your brother, but cut the words off, knowing them for the needless, the casually conceived hurt they would have been. But after all they *were* brother and sister, they had always felt and experienced so much in common.

He sought to strike some chord, to open the gate between

them so that he could speak to her.

'Frances, do you remember that time –'

She got up.

'No, Raymond, it's no good talking like that. You say you want me to be happy – yet I know you're trying to interfere in some way. You want to plan my life for me – just as, in other ways, Oliver does.'

At the mention of Oliver's name they both felt the shields and the parapets, the castle walls, melt away, leaving them naked and uncomfortable. And knowing what she felt, he could not say anything more; felt his incapacity to try and direct any other life, even her life, when his own was so lost, so rudderless.

And suddenly he was with her again, at her feet, wanting nothing any more except that she should remain there supporting him, sustaining him.

'Oh, Frances, forgive me. It's just that I sit and worry and think. I feel the world spinning round, I get a sense of disintegration. It's only that I want some things to remain solid, like rock.'

She smiled at him, wanly.

'Some things always do, always will. But perhaps not if you batter at them.'

They went, after a while, into the hall and sat down to the supper Edith had laid for the two of them. A third place was left ready for Oliver when he returned from a farmers' meeting. They ate, slowly and quietly, the cold salad, the slices of tongue, the flavour of the mayonnaise, the thick brown farm bread with salty butter; drank a glass of cider each. The fire was warm and friendly, the evening had drawn in and the big paraffin lamp was lit and humming away in the corner. There was a sense of timelessness, of nothing happening and nothing moving, and of a sort of emptiness.

Raymond sat there, in some ways at peace, yet never quite sure about her, as she gazed across the glass bowl and the flowers into the nearby fire. He thought, with a flash of bitterness – God, I suppose she's wanting to go out, to go down to that man in his wooden hut? Or perhaps she'd like me to go out so he can move in here? ... He bit at his lip, hating his mind racing away; it was her affair, it had nothing to do with him. It was her affair.

'All the same, you'll have to tell Oliver, won't you?' he said doggedly, and that was their only conversation for the rest of the meal.

*

'Make no mistake about it, mechanisation has come to stay and it is idle to deplore it.' The speaker paused, ran a hand through iron-grey hair, coughed, held up a hand for emphasis.

'I ask you, gentlemen. What has made possible the enormous increase in our food production? I will tell you. Machines. Tractors and combines. The tractor and the mechanical plough may not be as pretty to watch as a team of horses and the old two-furrow plough. But they do the same good job and do it infinitely quicker. Indeed, for myself I would go further, and suggest that there is even something thrilling about mechanised farming – something in its own way as beautiful as the old traditional methods.'

Another pause, another cough. Down the long British Legion Hall members of the Bedruthan Farmers' Union murmured the general agreement, taking their cue from the nods of the other speakers, seated round in a semi-circle on the platform.

'Be that as it may' – and the hand raised again – 'be that as it may, machinery is here. It is time that farmers and farmhands alike accepted this fact and set out to make the best of it. It is not machinery that is at fault, but our attitude to it. Not machinery that is wrong, but our misuse of it. We won't take the trouble to be machine-conscious. Why not? Doesn't it seem rather ridiculous, when we remember that the whole function of machinery is to increase output and ease the burden of heavy toil? Why, only last week, at a large agricultural research station in the West Country I saw ...'

Oliver sat behind the table, in the centre of the semi-circle, in front of him the writing pad, the fountain pen, the jug of water, all the prerogatives of the chairman, listening to the staccato enumeration of facts and figures. This was a clever speaker, this representative of one of the country's biggest combine harvester manufacturing firms, with his air of sweet reasonability, his expressive shrugging of the shoulder as he mentioned one massive achievement after another. His words were well received among the nodding heads.

'Surely we must agree that it is appalling to think of the sheer weight of material that has to be moved and lifted, again and again, on a farm during a year?'

In about ten minutes, he thought, looking at his gold watch, this speaker would end, and then it would be the chairman's duty to speak a few gracious words and introduce the opposer of the motion. He glanced sideways at the man on his left, a well-known writer and farmer in his own right who was notable, almost notorious, for his fierce opposition to any form of mechanisation in farming. He knew what Rawson would say. An era of great scientific advance was bound to upset the equilibrium of society. Since agriculture was the physical basis on which a civilisation was built, it must be the means of restoring this lost balance. It was only through a regenerated agriculture in which we returned to nature and followed her ways that we could begin to see a solution to the maze of economic problems that were such a discredit to our age. Then the frontal attack on the evils of mechanisation, of artificial fertilisation. The land must be tilled in small peasant holdings ... the village community to become again the basic form of social structure ... workers should be considered as craftsmen and artists ...

Oh yes, he knew what Rawson would say, for most of that evening he had talked with Rawson in a quiet corner of the Antelope. The fact was, in his heart, he knew that Rawson was right. Yet in the case of his own farm it was only by the aid of huge tractors and other machinery that he had cut his way over the country on the enormous land reclamation schemes that had made his farm a noted one in the county. How could he have done it otherwise?

He nodded and smiled with due modesty as the harvester

representative cited, in support of his case, some flattering reference to his own farm.

Yes, how otherwise? And yet: he frowned. And yet, he had been greatly disturbed by his encounter. For you could not deny the integrity of a man like Rawson. The very look of him, the strong brown face, the keen quizzical eyes, the unafraid way of meeting your eyes – it was impossible not to like and respect the man. Whereas, he knew, it was very possible not to like or respect the other man, who was now speaking with such elaborate verbiage on behalf of the great steel snorting dragons on which his livelihood depended. He could not help feeling that Rawson had got hold of some elemental truth when he said, as he had done to him earlier that evening, 'Your machine carries its own poison, my friend. You can plough up a billion acres in some miraculous time, but be very careful you don't lose something on the way.' And he had been held by something in the other's eyes, something in the tone of his voice, when he went on to say, 'It's not how much you do, what heights or distances you reach that matters. It's how you make the journey. Like that old saying about not seeing the wood for the trees – or, ends and means all over again.' And though they were ostensibly talking about farming he knew that Rawson saw it as a universal truth, and that he himself could not but see it as such.

Now the other speaker was finished, and he was on his feet introducing Rawson, listing his books, his qualifications, pausing for the polite applause to die away then quietly subsiding into his impartial seat while Rawson began speaking in his pleasant even voice, speaking truths that would be wasted on such an audience.

And as the quiet voice flowed on, gently and yet urgently, discreetly and yet challengingly, Oliver was surprised at the peace it gave him to sit and listen and absorb. A surprise that anything now should be able to bring him any sort of peace, or even reach through the strange turmoil of questioning, with which it seemed his mind was eternally possessed.

He took himself back to the evening about a week ago when he had seen Frances and Mark together, when the truth had dawned on him – not as a revelation, or even a shock, but as the slow climax to all the unease and haunting that had lain upon him for so many weeks. He remembered how he had got out of the car and walked away without exchanging another word with Raymond – how from then until now neither he nor Raymond had referred to what they had seen – how he himself had not referred to it with Frances, either. How, if only in order to give himself time to think, to regain his bearings, to gather up the suddenly scattered threads, he had pursued a grim course of normal life, a tight-rope existence of pretence.

He remembered awakening the next morning and sitting up in bed. The sunshine cut through the top edge of the windows and fell across the bed, touching the fringes of Frances' hair, lying around her like a pool of clear water. He sat looking down at her, lying there like some innocent child – she always, he felt, looked so young as almost to be a child again when she was asleep.

He felt a painful tenderness as his eyes took in, almost as etchings, the soft lines of her face, the long sweep of the eyelashes now cloaking from harsh reality those wide brown eyes that had been the first of her that he had ever seen; across a room, across a whole continent it might have been, and yet even then they had at once seemed real and familiar. The way she was lying now, turned to one side with her two arms out-stretched loosely, the clothes pushed down a little and showing the soft cream of her shoulders where the nightdress had slipped down – there was about her a strange impression almost of supplication, so that he felt an aching desire to bend down and gently embrace her.

And then, with a mixture of anger and despair, he dropped his hands to his side and turned away and got out of bed as if to hide his spontaneous loving desire, not only from her but from himself. For was there not now the black shadow between them, darkening all that white form, even though it lay there so serene and innocent, apparently so unshadowed?

He remembered going out that morning after breakfast, working in the cowshed with Mark, just as if it was any other morning. Walking round the sites and the stables and the chicken huts, attending a Ministry of Agriculture inspector while he checked up on the grains stores; finally collecting Mark from the stables and walking with him across to the potato fields to spend the morning on a final weeding. The strangeness of walking beside Mark, a foot away, no more, as they had walked so many mornings before, and of it being so much not the same, of it being another experience entirely. How odd, he had thought, to think of my saying only a few days ago to Mark – do you believe in marriage? How very odd. And at the oddity of it he had burst out laughing, a hollow, rough, but not unmirthful laugh – for indeed it did seem funny.

And he remembered the surprise with which Mark had eyed him, and the wary way in which he had returned Mark's look so that suddenly the German had looked away. He wondered then whether Mark knew that he knew, or whether it was just his own imagination. He found himself wondering, too, what Mark felt, whether he felt fear, or triumph, or whether perhaps he did not really care much.

It was this that surprised him most of all, in this strange no-man's-land period of his life – this reaction of intense curiosity, of detached analysis. He did not know whether to feel disappointed or pleased at the comparative absence of any of the conventional reactions, violence, anger, disgust, hatred ... He tried to consider honestly whether they were there within him, slumbering perhaps. For, good heavens, it would be a most natural thing for him to feel a tremendous, burning hatred, if not for Frances, for Mark, for this outsider, this worker stealing into his home, stealing into the heart of his life.

But even as he tried to follow the train of thought he came to the dead end, to the unavoidable wall. Frances had been apart from him for a long time, for a longer time than since Mark had come into her life. And out of the vacuum came a line he had once read in a work of philosophy, or perhaps in some magazine: infidelity is not a cause but a symptom. He found himself repeating the phrase over and over again. Infidelity is not a cause but a symptom, infidelity is not a cause but a symptom, is not a cause but a symptom, is not a cause but a symptom, – a symptom, symptom, symptom.

And so for some days he had gone about his work and the routine of daily life quite mechanically, outwardly unchanged. But it was like acting in some play of which you knew only so much and no more. All the time, while he performed the mechanical and recognised acts, he was secretly withdrawn into a self he had hardly bothered with before, he was considering the deep-down, unanswered riddle: Symptom of what? Symptom of what? What?

It isn't as if I've been an unfaithful husband, an inconsiderate husband, a cruel husband, he thought, sitting at the dinner table in the evenings, watching her over the bowl of fruit, watching her head bowed down as she sipped at her soup; with Raymond's dark head bowed at one side, with the empty space at the other, with his own soup steaming up in front of him and awaiting his attention – no, it isn't that I've been any of these things.

Or have I? he would think at some later time, when they sat by the fire drinking their coffees, each occupied with inward thoughts. Or have I? It was a difficult question to answer, and when he came to consider why it was difficult he grew to understand; that it was so because there were, indeed, two possible answers, that there was, in fact, the totally opposite one to that which he so readily gave. True, he had not been unfaithful, but he was beginning to get a peculiar impression that that was almost an unimportant point. And true, he had not been a cruel husband, he had never lifted a finger against Frances – why the idea was ridiculous, he could not have done so to save his life. So, in the conventional sense he could answer both those questions quite honestly in the negative.

But had he been a considerate husband? It was this question now that followed him about, in his work and at meals, in the morning and the afternoon, that he found himself repeating as he sat at the tractor, or worked up and down the long potato field, with Mark's fair hair bent low on the opposite side – had he been a considerate husband? He had always cared for her, always loved her, loved the children, provided a home, money – yes, yes, yes, these were all attributes of consideration. But was there something else?

Was there, indeed, something else?

And now, five, no six days later, he had not answered that question, he had found no way of escaping it and no way of answering it, he had got nowhere – except, perhaps, towards a sense of surprise that so much time of his mind should be occupied with those philosophisings and that he should hardly think about the immediate, horrifying reaction. Why, God, how did he know but that every moment he was not there, Frances was slipping out of the back door, down to the hut and Mark? – no, it was well not to think of it, there was nothing to be done about that or anything, not until his mind had resolved itself. For that matter (the thoughts slipped out despite his resolution) perhaps they made love under the very roof, in the library – but he would never know, never know. Once when, in a fit of despair, he burst into the library only to find it empty and desolate, he stood there trying to extract in some physical way its secrets: but was left empty and barren.

So there was no answer, he thought, stirring in his chair as if emerging from a dream, in time to hear Rawson's closing words, to see Rawson's warning finger held high as he warned them all against the folly of imagining that the land of their country could profitably be regarded as a mass production factory.

And he felt a rush of admiration for this man who had found for himself an answer, who held a faith and stood up for it and practised it. Getting up quietly, he said:

'Ladies and gentlemen, I am sure you will all have listened with great interest to Mr Rawson's viewpoint. It is what is perhaps regarded as a minority viewpoint, but I do not think any of us, in our hearts, can have failed to be struck by the deep truth of what Mr Rawson was expressing.

'Everyone here who is a farmer of long standing will already know, as those who are born and bred to it know intuitively, that farming is a way of life as well as a job. I doubt if there is one farmer in a hundred, no in five hundred, who will ever say flatly, I hate farming and I'll give it up tomorrow. He will grumble, yes, but that is the national pastime of farmers, at least according to our newspapers. But he goes on being a farmer.

'Ladies and gentlemen, perhaps that is what Mr. Rawson is getting at. Perhaps he is trying to remind us not to go too far in our applications of modern mechanisation for fear that in so doing we might change not only our method of farming but our way of life, that we might find ourselves suddenly factory owners instead of farmers of the plough and the four seasons – and perhaps too late, regret it.'

Oliver paused for a last breath, looking round quickly, as surprised as his hushed listeners at his flow of loquacity, seeking for the right words to end.

'For, and let me apologise at once in case there happens to be a factory owner present by mistake' – the murmur of laughter came softly – 'the fact is there is nothing in the world we farmers would dislike more than to be factory owners.'

Abruptly he sat down. For a moment here was an uncertain pause, and then slowly, but with cumulative effect, they clapped and cheered. Tomorrow they would go back to their same routine ways and methods, but tonight they had been moved by the words, they had been opened up a bit, and the seed of something might have penetrated. Suddenly aware how exhausted he was by his efforts he sank back into the chair, huddled up, yet in some way pleased. He had never moved an audience before in quite this way. But then he had never before been so emotionally stirred and upheaved himself.

'Well said,' murmured a voice beside him, quietly. He looked round quickly, almost nervously, and felt Rawson's grey eyes studying him.

He smiled.

'Oh, well, I expect it'll earn me some brickbats. I'll probably regret it myself tomorrow, when I'm sitting back on my trusty Fordson.'

'Nevertheless, you spoke from the heart. That is all that matters.' For a moment, for what seemed to Oliver a long moment of understanding, Rawson's eyes remained on him.

'I have enjoyed our talk this evening,' the older man said pleasantly. 'I hope we can perhaps resume it another time.'

'Indeed, yes,' said Oliver. 'I wonder – perhaps you would care to come out and look over my place?'

Rawson nodded.

'Very much.' He smiled. 'But not just now – a bit later perhaps? Because –' and his look now was almost affectionate in its wisdom – 'just now, if you will pardon my saying so, you give the impression of one who has some sort of problem on his mind – that is why, of course, you spoke so well tonight. I have had the same experience myself. Often a great inward conflict seems to soften us, to make us more human – out of this we strike out on new and truer pathways of our emotions.'

'Yes,' said Oliver slowly. 'Yes ...'

'A little later then?' said Rawson. He fumbled in his waistcoat. 'Here is my card – I shall look forward to hearing from you. In the meantime –' he got to his feet, a tall, well-built man with deep lines of experience engraved in his face, with a softened wisdom in his eyes, a man who could give someone as alone as Oliver a strange sustenance and direction – 'in the meantime, one thing may perhaps help you. It is simply that if we always try to speak with our heart, we shall not go far wrong in our search for truth, in our search for the right path and for the correct decision. Good night.'

*

It was raining when Oliver came out into the market square. The raindrops came down steadily in hissing patterns, pit-patting relentlessly on to the wet pavements so that you could be sure of no respite until after the next day's dawn. Tonight there was no Lagonda, it lay in silence in the barn while the battery was being charged, and he had to return by the last bus to the end of their lane and then walk the mile and a quarter to the farm.

He had cursed the rain when he first came out into it, but after leaving the bus with its chattering load of villagers bound for various isolated houses and farmsteads – once he was immersed into the silence of country night – he found a companionship in the swish of the rain, in the regular tapping of the raindrops on the smooth surface of his mackintosh. He walked along the lane at a fast pace, inhaling deep breaths, swinging his arms backwards and forwards, deriving a sensual pleasure from his swift movement through the silence and the dim mist of the rain.

He wished that Rawson was walking beside him, someone who could walk in silence but yet in understanding, someone to whom he could talk freely without expecting or needing a direct answer. He was conscious, with a frightening clarity that he had never known before, of the possible solitariness of his life. With the habit that was an absolute part of his character he had accepted Frances – their marriage, the children – into the permanency of life, just as he accepted as permanent the farm, the fields, the crops, every achievement of all his years. His loyalty to and acceptance of these things was real, he knew; and so, he had automatically supposed, was their permanency. Now the inevitable illusion of all permanency was revealed to him, jaggedly, a wound from which, at the first impact, one felt it was only possible to bleed to death.

It is like the rain, like the plants, like the earth, he thought morosely, nothing lasting, everything growing and then dying. Oh, but those were generalities, those were the massive structures of life and its rhythm – *this* was no generality, this was him and his life, him and his wife, him and his children and him home: the past and the future, time-bombed by an unpredictable present.

He wanted, striding now across the last field, with the wind blowing great gusts of rain about him as if trying to buffet him this way and that, to send him reeling and helpless – he wanted fiercely to erase the facts, to paint over the black, evil blob with a white paintbrush – oh, he wanted to do that, please God, he was only human, he wanted it all to be a dream, please God was that wrong? And in the dusk he had a sudden picture, not of God, but Rawson – Rawson looking down at him with his understanding, and saying: 'Look to the heart and follow that path …' And when he came to the familiar white gate, and beyond it the familiar, loved and worked-for outlines of the farm, the light in their window, the rustling familiar sounds of the hens and the cattle and the pigs, he felt a certain strength because he was throwing away the paintbrush and facing the view and the black blob. And he thought, dispassionately, this is all that I want; all I love and live for lies here; yet it may no longer lie here.

That was a situation and still not an answer, and yet he felt a lightening of his heart as he went on, on across the yard and up the stone steps. Still there was not the answer; but perhaps the beginning of one.

He went in to a silent hall, the fire still burning, his supper laid out, a note on the table telling him that Frances had gone to bed. He rejected the momentary angry suspicions that flooded over him, threw the paper into the fire and went and sat at his supper of cold meat and salad and cheese and biscuits.

He sat there for a long time, eating and sipping at some cider, staring across at the new logs that he had thrown on as they burned and sizzled, reddening and flaming upwards – they too, he reflected, were as impermanent as everything. It was a strange, detached hour, almost an exhilarating one, of completeness, of unexpected abandonment to the sense of being alone and absolute, so that at one point he walked over and stood by the fire and thought of a world in which he was without anyone or anything belonging to him, a mystic world in which one strode proudly across wide bleak moors of time and humanity, towards a horizon of a black cross.

But after a time it palled, and grew disturbing, and when he had warmed himself for the last time before the fire he drained his third glass of cider and went upstairs. He heard his footsteps padding neatly on the stairs, the only sounds in the sleeping house except for a faint movement he caught, as he reached the landing, from Raymond's room (his mind flicked for a brief moment to the other, the real solitary occupant, and a great pity welled up in him, banishing his own self-pity).

When he went in the light was on and Frances was sitting up in bed reading, with her glasses on. For a moment he reflected that she gave a glimpse of the not too distant middle years, when they would be forty and turning towards grey and white hairs; familiar yet companionable, that figment of the Press, the settled married couple. He frowned abruptly.

'Why, Oliver – you're all wet. Here, take those clothes off before you get your death of cold.'

He turned, surprised at the warmth of her voice. She slipped out of bed and came over, helping him out of the clothes which indeed, he now realised, were wet through.

'Here, steady.' He laughed. For a moment there was peace, an absence of the need for anything except that peace. He undressed and dried himself all over with a rough towel until his body was a bright red, then got into bed.

But now the peace was gone again. He felt it, lying there beside her, feeling her sitting there in some taut, preconceived position, as if she had been sitting there for some time waiting for him to come, as if – he did not know why, but he sensed it at once – she wished to speak to him. His heart sank.

She looked down at the book open on her lap, trying to focus the print so that she should steady her nerves as well as her mind. All that evening since Raymond had spoken to her at supper she had been trying to avoid the truth of his words and failing, trying to pretend to herself that there was no need for what she felt there must be a need, trying to avoid the inevitable, the obvious task. She must tell Oliver. And so she had come to bed early and undressed and sat in bed, at first in the dark and later with the companionship of the light, waiting with one ear strained for the sound of his returning footsteps, while her mind wrestled and struggled with those words, the particular and only words that could somehow say what she meant and at the same time reach through to that part, that deep down solid centre of Oliver with which she was irrevocably linked – so that he would understand.

'Oliver,' she said at last, out of a great silence.

But as he heard her say his name, as his ear caught all the tortured strain and effort behind her ejaculation of that single familiar word, he lost all his confusion of fear and distrust and unhappiness. The one, uncommunicative yet revealing word pierced him to the heart, was a cry from out of a loneliness as great in its way as his own.

And in the wonder of this understanding of how universal is all loneliness, and of the triviality of its different guises and appearances, he felt within himself a great, almost a new tenderness towards Frances. Shyly he reached a hand out until it was resting on hers, over the wide yellow coverquilt.

'Don't,' he said gently. 'There's no need to say anything. Better not, you'll only upset yourself.'

'But Oliver –'

'No! There's no need, Frances.' He swallowed uncomfortably. 'I know what you're going to say.'

'You do?' She looked at him quickly, held his eyes for a moment and turned away with a sigh.

'I've known for – a few days.'

'But you've said nothing.'

'What was there to say?' He had not meant it, but the faint inflection of self-pity was there. Catching it she hardened again.

'Oliver, it's difficult to explain. But one thing I must say – I'm not ashamed of anything.'

And because in that moment he was conscious of the depth, and even surprised at the strength of his own love for her, he was almost deaf to what she said, and could only see her lying there almost as a child again.

'Take your spectacles off, darling,' he said quietly, and when she did not stir he took them off with a gentle movement, and put them on the table.

'But Oliver, I want to try and explain –'

'Now kiss me good night. And then go to sleep. You're tired.'

The kiss was a fragmentary, gentle one, carrying in it possibly nothing, possibly everything.

He lay back and stared ahead to where the shadows on the edge of the candlelight were dancing on the wall. He did not expect he would sleep for some time, but he hoped she would. Once she made a movement as if to talk again, as if protesting, wishing to establish some fact, some idea. He pressed her arm gently, but insistently.

'There's nothing to talk about, darling. Or if there is let me do it some other time. You see, it's all rather a surprise to me. It may take me some time to get my bearings. It's odd, but I *am* getting them.'

He heard her whisper come softly, tearfully, out of the great gulf, the enormous space that must now separate them.

'Oliver, can you understand – I do love you. It's only that –'

He waited till her words had dried up into silence.

'Do you, darling?' he said slowly, wonderingly, a question to himself more than her.

Do you, darling? he thought incessantly, hour after hour, that long and lonely night, while she slept restlessly beside him. Perhaps and perhaps not. It was now like the game with the fluffy flower, whatever it was called, the one with white petals which you blew upon and wished. She loves me, she loves me not.

But somewhere in the mystery of the night he came to realise that like all problems it had two possible answers, and that as with all problems the decision was not fore-arranged, but depended entirely on the pattern of behaviour – depended upon him as much as upon her.

And with that thought, at once an addition to his understanding and a challenge to his weary impotence, he actually fell asleep.

VIII

The party of visiting farmers came early after lunch. Oliver met them in Bedruthan with Daker, his local NFU president, and then they had a stand-up lunch in the Antelope before cramming into the Lagonda and Daker's more sedate Austin for the short journey to the farm.

They were a cheerful and inquisitive group: three farmers from Midland counties, a sheep farmer from the Lake District, the farming correspondent of an evening newspaper covering a large agricultural area in Derbyshire, and a rather blustery Yorkshire retired business man who had taken up farming as a hobby and boasted of working the largest acreage in North England.

'Ah, and 'twould surprise me to hear of any bigger down your way,' this man said with a challenging look at Oliver.

Oliver liked the contact, the meeting of north and south, learning something of methods of farming which seemed to vary in subtle details, county by county. The party was being sent on a goodwill tour by the northern branches of the NFU; in return, later, a group from the south would go round northern district. Daker had already suggested to Oliver that he might like to be one of the members, but Oliver had declined firmly.

The truth was, he thought, ushering his guests into the farmyard, pointing to the new stables and calling out for Bailey to come and exhibit a particular prize horse, the truth was his mind could hardly grasp farming at all. It was fortunate that the farm was in good running order, events ticking over in regulated progress, for if anything had come to a standstill he would have felt simply without strength to restart. It was partly physical: he had taken to going on long tramps around the farm estate, ostensibly to inspect hedges and ditches, but in reality to give himself time to think. And that was even wearying, the strain of mental toil. It seemed that he must have deluded himself in the past in assuming that he led an intelligent mental life. Now he felt the entire pattern of his life suddenly isolated and adrift, like an icefloat, and with it the method of his thinking and the nature of his conclusions.

In the cowshed, swept bright and spotlessly clean for the special occasion, though it was very neat and hygienic, he showed the visitors the mechanical milking apparatus, the patent fixtures for speeding up the milking, the new sluicing channels.

Once upon a time he would have been eager and excited, like a father showing off a child, an inventor his toy. But now he was miserably conscious of his lack of interest, at pains to cover it up with a false joviality that he felt could deceive no one except perhaps the Yorkshire businessman.

'And through here are the sties,' he said. 'It might interest you to see them. Then I thought we might take a stroll round the fields – all reclaimed from wasteland.'

'That's right, Mr Williams,' said the farming correspondent. 'I've heard quite a lot about your land reclamation. I must mention that in my articles. We have plenty of wasteland up our way – more than round here. But it's a terrible job to get farmers on to it. They'd rather make do with the cultivated land they've got. You tell them it's short-sighted and they just shrug.'

'Oh well, I hope if you tell them about my experience they might change their minds,' said Oliver. 'For believe me, it's a job worth doing. There must be thousands of acres in this country lying waste. Land that could be giving food and milk. There's no doubt in my mind but that we could be a self-supporting nation, agriculturally.'

'Really?' said the journalist with interest. He took out his notebook. 'You won't mind if I quote you for that?'

'No, please do,' said Oliver. 'I'm anxious to help all I can to

Frances 147

make people land-development conscious.'

What words, what words are these, he thought inwardly, hearing his voice almost with surprise, as it went on metallically with facts and figures. Who was he to say he was anxious about land development? – when the truth was in his whole world and life he was only anxious now about one thing, that was all that mattered to him; his wife and their marriage.

It appalled him to realise on what sandy foundations his whole apparent everyday life was based, to realise how little everything else had mattered beside this single heart-felt problem. All he knew now was that he – whose life was apparently dedicated to the task of reclaiming the land, building one of the biggest farms in Cornwall, spreading his power and the land further and further – cared not one jot if the whole farm blew up, atomwise, the next moment.

And yet it also humbled him, so that he shuddered with impotent rage against his stupidity, his insensitivity, his blindness – against his presumption in taking such a vast landscape and canvas for granted, as permanent. He remembered the days when he first met Frances, the times of their courtship, the early years of their marriage, and he knew that there had been a fullness and a richness about it. But when he tried to trace a pathway from then onwards, and to do so from a detached position, he was forced again and again to the anguished conclusion that the faults had been his. It was he who had failed, he who had gradually forgotten to be a lover, then even to be a true husband, he who allowed himself to become immersed in a whole series of external superficial ideas and objects – so much so that they had come to form a pattern which was a way of life.

He thought back now with a fascination that became horror, turning back the pages and remembering the hard, rigid purpose of his life, the all-importance to him of the farm and the acreage and the work, morning noon and night, thinking always about it, becoming supplicant to it, dominated by it – how little, beside it, had really mattered Frances and the children! Oh, superficially, yes – but his mind at bottom had taken them for granted, had considered itself free to devote its real attention elsewhere – to tractors and ploughs and seeds and crops – oh! he could curse the whole lot to damnation.

'And how many fields of corn have you laid, Mr Williams?' asked the Yorkshireman argumentatively.

He swallowed hard, bringing himself back to the reality that was no longer the reality, supplying the meaningless figures. For the first time he took a good look at the Yorkshireman and felt a deep hatred for this businessman who had come to the land with all his money and machines and his ideas drilled and trained in some long shining metallic factory – who was trying to machine the land like some vast industrial plant. What the hell did it matter how many fields of corn this lout had planted with a host of mechanical aids? He, Oliver, would give ten times more worth to the modest twenty-acre farm of the little wizened Warwickshire farmer whose family had farmed for generations and who knew the real truth and fundamentals of farming.

Abruptly he pulled himself up, surprised. A thought had struck him, a horrible thought. He saw a vision of himself in ten years' time if he pursued his present ambitions, and what he saw was almost identical to the big blustering northern farmer beside him – why, God, he would become like that, that would be Oliver at fifty! Suddenly he knew how piercing and how warning was the vision, and he had to turn away to avoid anyone seeing the spasm of horror that contracted his face.

For here was the acid and the poison that had corroded his life – here, he suddenly understood, was the twist and the precipice that had loomed apparently out of nowhere. He had been rushing like some wild tornado into a barren future, away from the very things that were really the basis of his life. Away from the love and the understanding that were the lifeblood of any marriage; away from Frances.

He supposed it was an odd moment, in the middle of a conducted tour of his farm, emerging from pigsties and outwardly commenting on the quality of the straw – an odd moment to reach a momentous conclusion of this nature.

So odd that he could not help a faint smile, and it was on his face until he saw Mark standing in the gateway across the yard, watching them curiously – until he saw Mark's form filling the gateway with arms outstretched, his silhouette a barrier to the way out.

And in the savage despair of the moment the smile froze like ice on his face and he shouted roughly:

'All right, Mark, no need to lounge about. Be on with your work!'

As if he were telling off some urchin schoolboy. It was the first time, in fact, he had ever spoken a harsh word to the German who was an excellent worker, anyway, considerably better than his own permanent hand, Bailey. And it had been spoken unfairly, he knew. But God knows, I have every right to say much worse things to the swine, he thought, unleashing the awful bitterness in a wave, yielding himself up for a moment to the forbidden drug, daring to do so because he could see with clarity, the painful but only way of recovery, of resurrection – and in that way there was no room for hatred of Mark, only of himself.

Now they filed out into the fields, down among the great squares of green sprouts and blue-grey cabbages. At the far end he took them beyond the tractor's path into the wild no-man's-land out of which he had fashioned the farm, and watched their faces with grim pride as they realised what efforts and energies must have been expended on cutting the pattern of neatness out of such a jungle. Even the Yorkshireman's face showed a merited respect.

On the way back Daker, walking beside him, pointed down to the reservoir.

'I see you've got gipsies.'

He frowned, shading his eyes.

'Where?'

Daker pointed to the faint blue curl of smoke coming out of a wooded copse.

'Better keep an eye on them. We've had a lot of trouble lately. They've probably been helping themselves to your vegetables, if not one or two fowls.'

'The devil they have!'

All the pent-up bitterness and resentment that he had been

allowing to bubble, thinking it safe and under control, now welled up like a river that has been dammed and suddenly finds a new outlet.

'The devil they have!' he repeated angrily, staring across to the wood. 'I'll soon put a stop to that.'

'Ah, do,' said Daker. 'Can't abide them myself. Vagrants and rascals. There ought to be a law against them.'

'I'll go down to them as soon as you're gone,' vowed Oliver with unexpected heat, so that Daker glanced at him in surprise. He laughed.

'Well, don't do anything rash. But you're in your rights to demand they leave your land. And they'd have to go a good way then. Perhaps once they start on the move they'll clear out of the district.'

Gipsies, he thought, cashing in on my land, stealing crops. It's not right, I'll send them packing. He bit his lip and fumed all the way back, and was quite impatient for the party to finish its visit.

But first there had to be a simple politeness, a cup of tea in the big hallway and some of Frances' home-made nut and fruit cake, with Edith wearing her best apron and handing round, Timothy and Theresa watching round-eyed from the couch and Raymond staring with dark sarcasm from an isolated corner by the fire. He smiled as he remembered Raymond's mimicking the local farmers that evening – when was it? A century ago it seemed. His eyes came to rest on Frances, her red lips parted and her face flushed, looking radiant as she passed among the guests inquiring for more tea cups, the picture of the farmer's smart and attractive wife ...

He could imagine how they would comment later, lucky fellow, that Williams, to have such a lovely wife. Seeing the radiance and knowing in his heart that it sprung from something outside of them and their marriage, something part of her life but not of his, he felt an anguish and despair sweeping over him, momentarily obliterating all his cold logic and self-analysis of the afternoon. Oh, God! He wanted to groan, he wanted to sit down and weep ... It would have been a great relief, but a greater indulgence, to lose control; and somehow he bottled up the unshed tears and the lonely despair into a cold anger directed against the blue smoke and the impudent gipsies. By God, I'll have them off the land by nightfall, he vowed.

And no sooner had the farmers gone, with many kind words and salutations, than he came back into the hallway and collected his coat.

'Off to work?' said Raymond, lazily.

'Yes – well, not exactly. Going down to send some gipsies packing.' He hesitated. 'Care to come?'

He was relieved when Raymond declined. Somehow he had wanted it to be a personal and single thing, to act on his own without obligations to others. Yet, for some reason, he carried with him out of the door a curious image of Raymond's face sagging, inexorably wearied, as if he had had some shock or other. He almost turned back to inquire, 'Not feeling well, old man?' as he would have done any other time. But not this particular time. He had a mission and an itch to express his helpless anger.

He picked up an old walking stick as he went out through the porch and tucked it under his arm. You never knew with gipsies – his father had once been half-killed by a wild gipsy youth who went for him with an axe. It had been an occasion not unlike this; he remembered it well from the mists of his childhood as if some peculiar significance must always have belonged to it. The gipsies had been seen by one of the farm-hands stealing some chickens. The next day his father had met one of them in the lane outside the village and started giving him a piece of his mind. While they were still arguing another of them, the young one, had run up and clubbed his father on the back of the head with the blunt end of an axe. They had hit and kicked him, and finally stolen all his money, then disappeared leaving him unconscious in the gutter. The young one had been caught and given five years' imprisonment.

For a moment, gripped by this echo of drama, he forgot his other worries, thought only about the gipsies and their blue smoke – was conscious of the cold shock of surprise at the thought that perhaps he, too, was going out towards violence, pain, perhaps death?

Slipping the walking stick down to his hand he flicked viciously at the cowslips and nettles trailing the edge of the hedges. He was in a mood for it all, he thought, with an almost masochistic pleasure.

But when, walking briskly across the fields and the long reservoir path, he came at last to the small clearing in the wooded copse, he found the caravan deserted and silent, the ground heaped with smouldering ashes of a fire not long since dampened down. He frowned: there was no way they could have known of his impending visit. If they had seen him only as he crossed the wide reservoir path there would have been no time to put the fire out.

He poked around, looking under the caravan, peeping through one of the windows into the surprisingly neat interior – floral red and blue designs along the wall, lace net curtains, a long table, a wall couch, at the back two layers of beds, one above the other. The iron fire-place opposite the window through which he was looking had a bright-gleam about it. It was a clean, very clean caravan. He was mildly surprised, always associating gipsies with rags and dirt and bundles of wooden pegs.

He went back to the fire and poked at its centre with his walking stick, raising a tiny spiral of smoke that curled upwards with tortuous efforts, as if wanting only to succumb to the silence of death. He watched it with growing fascination, his eyes following each spinning curl round and round, up and up, until he could almost believe the smoke was putting on a performance especially for his benefit – as if, almost, it was mocking him, saying, Look, here am I, nothing but embers, and yet I can rise up and up and up.

When the smoke had reached the height of his own eyes he swung the stick down with a savage crack into the centre of the embers, scattering them in all directions, lopping off the whole pattern of the smoke column.

He was still bending forward, pressing the stick end hard into the burnt centre – still exalting in the moment of satisfied fury – when he became conscious of the girl standing in front of him.

He looked up slowly. She was standing at the other side of the fire, a young, very young gipsy girl with thick dark hair hanging around her shoulders and pushed back from her head by a yellow scarf. She had a pale face in which the dominant feature was the two deep brown eyes. In the eyes was all the early maturity and wisdom of the nomad races; in the soft mouth, the slender throat and the shape of her beneath her tight black dress was all the freshness and promise of the young and the innocent.

The consciousness of the girl's pallid tension communicated itself to him so that he felt himself trembling, whether with nervousness or irritation he could not be sure.

'What do you want?' she said at last.

'I want you off my land,' he said roughly.

'Oh, I thought –'

'You'll have to think again.'

He jabbed the stick into the embers, looking downwards as he spoke.

'The reservoir is public property, but the land all round it, including this copse, belongs to me. Tregonna Farm, up there on the hill.'

'Nobody told us that.'

The girl's voice was sullen, her face hard; he could see her retiring into stubbornness. His temper flared up.

'Of course not! Because you took damn good care not to ask! Anyone round here would have told you this was my land. I expect you've tried everywhere else and no one will have you, so you come creeping down here. Well, I'm not having you either. You can be on your way. Do you understand?'

He was surprised at his own harshness, at the hardening of his voice. He could not have imagined being more unpleasant to some lifelong enemy.

'Well, it's no good telling me. You'll have to tell my father. He's away in the village, he and my mother.'

'Oh, he is, is he?' Oliver fumed. 'And I suppose I'm to stand here and just wait patiently until your father takes it into his head to come home. Now look here, young woman, I'm not in the best of tempers –'

'I can see that,' said the girl insolently.

He gripped the knob of the stick tightly, his knuckles white to the bone. God, if she were a man he would have whipped the stick across her back.

'And don't be rude either. You've no right here!' he cried, with a sudden desperate rise of his voice, as if seeking to drown other voices. 'Why don't you get on your way? Why do you come bothering me, making trouble, probably stealing my cattle …'

They stood facing each other across the fire, like two antagonistic animals held in the grip of some strange tension so that neither could break from the pattern of behaviour and movement. He felt his voice rising higher and shriller; and even as he uttered the words and threats he was overwhelmingly conscious of what a fool of himself he was making, of the madness and wildness, even the unfairness of his epithets.

And it was just then, just when he was at the height of his stream of words, just as the girl opposite him seemed to grow tense and white, her eyes looming larger and brighter as if bulging with tears, or so he supposed – just then that the taut wire seemed to snap, the harsh canvas dissolve, and as he watched he saw the girl's white face loosen and the mouth open with a wide sensual smile – so blatant and unashamed, so obvious and deliberate, as almost to be wicked, were it not, as he knew by some intuition, perfectly natural and logical.

As they stood there for a moment more, the girl smiling that slow, secret smile, her eyes seeming to melt into the rest of her, he was conscious of some strange inner change, as if his whole emotion had inexplicably reversed – as if, indeed, it had taken some twisted turning, because he was in a twisted state, because – because – and then he could think no more because he was conscious, and this time with a greater shock and urgency than that with which he had contemplated death and violence – conscious of the white, rounded girl opposite him, and above all of the overwhelming, simple and uncomplicated desire stretching between them as definitely as the tension and hatred

– but somehow more rightly.

At that moment the girl whirled round and before he could say anything she was padding away quickly towards the wood.

'Hey!' he cried. 'Stop!'

But at his words the girl broke into a run and disappeared among the trees.

With an exclamation he bounded over the fire and ran after her, plunging into the green and gold maze of the woods as if into some fairy grotto.

He heard the crackling of leaves and twigs under her feet, saw her ahead of him twisting and darting along the path.

'Hey!' he cried, and his voice echoed in and out, backwards and forwards among the tall trees. 'Stop! Wait!'

And then he heard another echo, the echo of her laughter, a wild rippling sound running right through the wood like some secret stream, and he stopped shouting, aware of having, in some subtle way, already entered into the girl's secret mood and life – suddenly unworried, suddenly happy, because it was a game and would end happily.

When they came to the side of the reservoir, to the last slope out of the wood, she allowed him to catch up with her.

The girl sank down breathless, bending her head forward so that her black hair spread all around her, hiding her face from him. He knelt down beside her, gently putting his arms around her, exhilarating at the feel of her hidden warmth and youth, suddenly feeling a youth again himself. He did not stop to think, or even want to think; he was conscious only of being no longer burdened with a mind and with prejudices, with the morose accusations and counter-accusations of his other world. He felt, through his hands, the laughter beating through the girl's entire body, like waves in the sea, and felt it somehow entering into him – as if their bodies were just for that moment, just for that afternoon, so much in harmony and tune that they felt the same things, that they experienced the same experience. He, too, began laughing, in slow chuckles.

And when he did that the girl looked up at last, their faces close together, so close together that there was a moment of fear, of being deluged and drowned. And then suddenly there was no more fear or wondering, suddenly their laughter and their wide open mouths were lost among each other, suddenly the storms and fires that smouldered within them both, from whatever different sources, burst open and fused into a common exhilaration and ecstasy. Suddenly they were lost and a part of the earth and the grass and the trees and the flowers.

And suddenly they were at peace.

A long time afterwards, as they lay there in the sleep of the afternoon sun, he stared at the girl's face, half turned away from him, the mouth open and soft, the eyes quietly closed, and he thought, there she lies, she is contented and happy; and he thought, and that must be how I look, here I lie contented and happy; and because he was a man and not a woman, his mind went on further, and he began thinking, how extraordinary that now there is about me no weight, no burden, nothing except a great peace and a great happiness. And yet I have no cause at all for either, really.

And then, as he shifted himself slightly and looked away into the deep blue mystery of the sky, it seemed to him that out of that inexplicable afternoon he had grown many more years in his wisdom.

For he knew as surely as ever he had known that he loved Frances as the great love of his life, and yet here he had been made happy by and had made happy this dark-eyed gypsy girl, and without any regrets. So there was born in him some understanding of the generosity and the width and the inexhaustibility of love, and at the same time there was destroyed all the immense barriers, the high castle walls, the uncrossable moat, that he had imagined had grown up between him and Frances because of Mark. For was it not that Frances might feel what he felt now when she turned to Mark? – this delightful sense of giving and taking, of something positive, something creative?

A great tenderness crept upon him. Gently he raised his hand and tilted the girl's chin towards him. Through the half-closed eye lids he saw the unfamiliar glitter of her eyes. Almost like an animal's eyes, he thought – and once again he was reminded of the isolation of these gipsies, of their estrangement from ordinary life as he knew it.

'Are you happy?' he said. The words sounded banal and artificial. He felt that words between them were unnecessary, even undesirable.

He bent forward and kissed her gently on each eye, as if to set a seal on the sense of peace that pervaded him and, he felt sure, her.

Once again they fell into drowsiness, comforted and no longer disturbed by the contact of their bodies, his fingers running lazily in the dark curtains of her hair. He was fascinated, a little awed, at her presence, so much a symbol, so much real and yet unreal.

'Where do you come from?' he asked, half to himself, and without waiting for an answer he went on. 'And where will you go? You will wander and wander, I suppose. A few days here, and a few days there, never at peace and yet, at least, never at war. An hour ago I despised your way of life, or at least disapproved. Now it seems to me different, I see about it the good things, the freedom and the expansion, the widening experience – above all, the endurance, the imperishability. You and your kind are perhaps the reflection of a secret part of us … you exist because that secret part must always exist. You wander restlessly, because a part of us must always wander restlessly, into the unknown.'

He smiled down at the girl, her eyes now open and watching him steadily.

'You probably hardly understand a word I'm saying. And yet, in another way, you do. You are wise, er – Fancy, I don't even know your name.'

'Does it matter? A gipsy girl – it is enough.'

He nodded.

'Funny – how we both know that. I wonder –' He hesitated.

Suddenly the girl pulled his head closer. She spoke into his ear, almost shyly.

'I have made you happy?'

He touched the lobe of her ear.

'Of course. Of course. Very much so.'

The girl stretched herself luxuriantly, turning her hands

outwards, as if to the sun.

'And you – too?' He felt the shyness enter into his own voice. When the girl nodded dumbly, he was inordinately pleased. For now it seemed to him one of the great truths of the world that in the moment was contained everything, and that accepting this, everything fell into one enormous, uncomplex pattern. For how many millions and millions of moments must there be in a life – and how wonderful a thing it would be to make each one so rich and creative, to fill each one with the giving of pleasure and renewal, of experience and development, of wisdom and understanding. It was as if he had been examining life on the wrong set of scales, arranged in a mistaken pattern, the horizontal instead of the vertical.

He was aware of the impossibility, perhaps the crime, of endeavouring to pin life down to a matter of two people cut off from other people. It was rather each person in relation to many people – the coming together of two might be a large part of that relationship but it would never be the whole. Otherwise you could not rationally explain a woman's love for her children, a brother's for a sister, a friend's for a friend. And you saw then, like the opening of a door, the simplicity of a creative worthwhile life and love – that it could fit to no rules precisely because it was inexhaustible, that everything given from the heart and spontaneous was always good.

And as his mind travelled over these thoughts he felt a new and deeper understanding of Frances, of the nature and necessity of her fulfilment. He thought of her and Mark with a new sympathy, almost a tenderness. And with the same tenderness he turned again to the dark eyes of the gipsy girl who, however unwittingly and accidentally, had brought him this freedom and wisdom.

'I wish I could tell you –' he began, and faltered.

The girl raised a finger and pressed it gently against his lips. 'We loved, we were happy. It is enough.'

'Yes,' he said slowly. 'Yes.'

And a little later, as they walked slowly away from the reservoir through the amber light of the woods, he felt a sweet sadness, for he knew without it ever being said that the next day the gipsies would go, the wanderers would drive on into the unknown. What had happened would vanish eventually, for both of them, into the mists of memory. But what it had released, and perhaps redirected, would remain with him for ever.

IX

Raymond saw them long after they had disappeared back into the woods, saw the two of them sitting there on the opposite bank, lost in a world of their own that might as well have been the other side of the Atlantic as of the short silver water of the reservoir. For him they had been there for ever, symbols of the inaccessible, dark shadows of the impotency of his life – growing up across his horizon like two jagged trees from which he could not take his gaze, at which he must stare until the last chalky bleach of the sky had been obliterated by the evening clouds.

He stirred only when the evening dusk enveloped him, shrouding the opposite bank, hiding much of the water, leaving him alone with the silence and the greedy lap-lap-lap of the little wavelets against the stone parapet. His body was cold and stiff, his eyes sore and puffed out from staring. He stood up and turned his back quickly on the evil wink of the water, lest it submerged him in its tears – lest its proximity drew out his own tears, sprung up in him like a mountain of sorrow. He began shivering, at first slowly, and then in short rapid movements, so that he stood there shaking in the night breeze like some lonely tree; aware of this shivering as if it were the experience of some detached being.

He had an odd sensation of standing away from himself, of watching himself, and thinking: Look at that poor fellow, standing there and shivering in the wind, how cold he must be, what a gaunt unhappy fellow he looks, what hollow eyes he has got, what dank and deathlike hair he has, how dark and sad he looks, how dripping with the sadness, as if he had stepped up from the dark depths of the water – as if he would be happier if he but stepped back into the darkness and oblivion. And he began to believe that perhaps he had, indeed, come from out of the water, perhaps in some curious way he had been spermed and conceived, had been born out of the wide surging womb of the water, a child of the fish-strewn mystery of water.

He might have felt the impact, the secret calling of the water too overpowering to resist, had not there appeared out of the darkness ahead of him a bright winking light, as someone lit the lamps in the big farmhouse on the hill. The light struck into his consciousness like a word from a helper; he was reminded of the only remaining root of him, a small box-room of twelve feet by twenty feet – the last refuge that (he now forgot) was never quite so.

An urgency descended upon him to reach his room, to seek some shelter before the storm of what he had seen, the thunder and the bitter lightning, came up again out of the temporary shock of oblivion. He turned and shambled along the towpath, not seeing properly where he was going, catching his feet in potholes, once falling forward and plunging his hands through the thick slimy mud. He stopped for nothing, scrambling up and onwards, running most of the time – while his breath caught sharply, while his heart pounded its thunder – but afraid to look behind him, for fear of some ghostly searchlight that might strike from the heavens and bathe in its golden glitter that cursed spot upon the opposite bank, scarleting its revelation.

When he reached the farm he was wet and mud-stained, but he sought no warmth, no comfort, only the secret solace of his room. He went in by the kitchen door and managed to slip upstairs unseen, tip-toeing all the way for fear of arousing some unwelcome attention.

In his room he locked the door and stood quite still, his whole body sagging. Then, slowly, as much dramatically as naturally, he fell forward on to the bed, spreadeagled, his arms outstretched and clutching at the coverlet: so that, as he could not help thinking, he was like a man crucified – but with his back to the light.

And so it was meant to be. Now he knew, pressing his knuckles and his arms, his tensed face, deep into the blinding coverlet. Everything in his life was meant to breed just this simple realisation: whatever his fingers touched would crumble away, whatever his eyes feasted on would vanish.

All the evening and most of the night, he lay there without stirring, careless of anything except the racing rhythms of his mind, pounding and tearing its way across the great oasis and the interweaving jungles of his life. For a long time he forced and wheedled and coaxed himself into not thinking about Oliver, or about anything of the present, thrusting his mind back and back, seeking always some spark of light, some forgotten morsel of reality to confront the granite wall of the reality of his failure. And then, when all that had failed, he allowed the sinews of his mind to rewind their track and to curl around the simple seizable prey: Oliver, I will hate you, Oliver, I will tear the heart out of you, Oliver, I will bring the heavens in frenzy upon you, Oliver – you who have walked across my life and obliterated its horizon for ever.

And as he thought these thoughts he groaned and stirred slightly, and his mind rolled over and over in turmoil and anguish. For it could not fight away the prodding, hurtful voice of reality: he knew deep down that it was not Oliver but himself, knew in his heart now as always that what Oliver had done he would never, never have done, that the barrier that was not there for Oliver's life was one side of the tight-rope and his own another, that Oliver must always ultimately walk into the sun but for him there was only the dark shadows of the pit and the cold gleam of the moon for comfort. It was as if every time he had looked at the gipsy girl it had been through a wall of glass, built brick by brick with his own hands, created out of his own mind, and now unerasable, unforgettable.

He groaned and moved his head from side to side. No, Oliver, I cannot hate you. And his mind darted away and upwards and downwards and sideways and forwards and backwards, seeking some rock again on which to hang, thinking with fear of the crumbling and the disintegration. But when he thought of Frances it was a cold and a fearful thought, under a shadow: he suddenly remembered Mark and his heart contracted. The whirlpool of Oliver and Frances and the children and Mark and the farm and the reservoir fell upon him, spinning round and round and round. Voices were crying out but he could not hear them, only guess at them … the whirlpool receded and then sprang into a shape, and the shape was Mark. He saw the broad, square head, and the fair hair, heard the guttural accent, and he shrieked in shocked silence: I hate you, Mark, I hate you, German, German, whom I should have killed when I was a coward.

And then, in the dark early hours of the morning, he felt himself inflated with a tremendous hate, and hate brought the sense of courage. He thought, I am not frightened of you, Mark, I am not frightened of Germans any more. But I hate you, Mark, you have brought ruin and disintegration upon this house, you have come like the invading army and brought blood and ruin and dejection and the splitting asunder of what had a meaning and a value to me, of my life and my roots. Mark, how dare you! I hate you, hate you, hate you! And now at last the tears were released because there was the torrent of bitterness to burn them out, and they sank like stone daggers into the bed coverlet.

Then perhaps he fell asleep, an uneasy sleep of that night underworld which haunts all solitary spirits. For into his sleep the isolated one takes the images of all those worlds and peoples from which he is so much removed, whereas the contented and companioned one shares them in his everyday life and may sleep at peace and alone.

And it seemed to Raymond, in his sleep, that he awoke into a room that was dark as the night, dark as the deepest pit. When he looked around he could not be sure whether what he saw were vague shapes belonging to the room, or merely huge, shapeless shadows. When he tried to move he became confused and frightened. He had a curious feeling that his limbs were moving, yet that he himself was not moving. Yet he was conscious, as if of the rapier thrust of fire, of the touch of his hands on the darkness.

It seemed that while he lay there in drowsy immobility

another part of him, his short, stubby fingers, travelled out into an unknown world, prodding its elastic mystery. Prodding ... prodding ... but reaching to what? His fingers, clawlike, pressed only into the depthless, empty darkness. It must be a very large room, he thought, and the darkness clung and tugged at his arms, damp on the flesh of his hands, cold to the tips of his fingers. Yet, somehow, so dark was the darkness, so large and empty and unresponsive was the room, it was quite impossible for him to know whether he was in fact moving his arms, or whether it was the darkness and not him that moved.

The blind must feel like this, he thought, awakening among strange surroundings, bereft of familiar sights and vistas, groping into the unknown, wanting desperately to touch a cornerstone of reality. And though he did not think he was blind, he began to think about blindness because now it seemed real and was something to cling to, a guidance, a precedent. He was the blind, groping in the unfriendly outer world. If he groped long enough and far enough he would find something. Even the blind found a way through the darkness.

Even a room must have walls, he thought, must have a roof and a floor, must have windows and a door, he thought with cunning. Must have walls, he thought, and swung his steel-sprung arms backwards and forwards, swinging to and fro and to and fro like great pendulums. Must have roof and floor, he thought, reaching his arms high up into the sky, then pounding them down like hammers into the earth. Must have windows, he thought, clawing with long dagger fingernails for the strangling curtain and the blue glass panes. Must have door, he thought, pulsing his muscles and smashing angry fists into the iron-bolted darkness ...

The great emptiness broke and fell about him in a hundred pieces, only to form its new shapelessness beyond his reach. And now he felt fear, for there were gathering shadows nearer to him than the darkness, stabbing at his calmness with a prick, prick, prick, like slow cold drips of water ... Faces that he recognised, moments that he could never forget, accusations that he could not answer ... all tumbling and swirling around him, like gigantic, twisting prison bars.

To be alone in a dark room, to be swamped and drowned in emptiness, to be imprisoned forever with one's own failure – no, cried his sleeping heart, no it was not possible. Somewhere, somehow there was a pathway – somewhere, somehow, somewhere, somehow, drummed his heart. Somewhere, somehow there was a door – somewhere, somehow, somewhere, somehow sang his memory. Somewhere, some-how there was a light – somewhere, somehow, somewhere, somehow, whispered his will.

And so it came to him, in his forgotten sleep, came to the blind, came to the lost one – came with a flash, the vision that beyond every darkness was a light, that for each one, though the darkness and the light might be of a different shape and purpose and meaning, yet the attainment was the same for all – that it was the simple one of a journey instead of a retreat, of a movement instead of inertia, of an effort instead of a despair. And in that deep sleep of the mind, in that dream like a child again, Raymond strode forth into the darkness and into the face of the yawning pit and the drowning seas, strode on and on, and saw at the end of it a great shining star, riding high and higher, unquenchable, like the sun.

But when he awoke he remembered only the nightmare and not the vision. When he awoke there was the grey tinge of dawn to make the world seem even more frightening and cold and grim, and the tiny shadows of light filtering into the room seemed to impart to it a reality of horror far greater than the darkness of the dream. He jumped up from the bed with a cry and stood in the centre of the room like a distraught creature, twisting this way and that, seeing all around him the dust and the ashes of his destitution and his failure – until, whimpering, he darted to the desk and seized the lazy heaps of manuscripts and hurled them into the air to fall like careless snow.

Now he felt all around him the falseness and the insecurity of this last unreal refuge, now he felt himself forced into the open and the inescapable, like the hunted fox. Shivering slightly he went to the window and threw it open wide, to stare out into the grey-gold portrait of a new day.

And suddenly, staring as he had stared every morning over

to the blue-smoked sign of the gipsies' camp, he noticed that this morning there was no smoke and knew that the inevitable had happened. At the realisation, the last vestige of his control and his restraint fell away from him like a cloak, and he wept like a child.

Still weeping, he fled, fled from the room that was a box and the house that was not real, out into the cold morning and the dewy soft turf – fled down the wide surprised fields and along the muddy towpath, treading back upon his own footsteps, only this time hurrying with the urgency of the too-late, too-late, too-late.

He reached the far end of the reservoir as the sun had pierced into the sky like three-quarters of a rich orange – as the birds and the trees, the flowers and the grass, the very air of the world were aglow with daybreak. From where he was he could look down upon the winding village road, and he saw, as he had expected, the trundling shape of the green-and-yellow gipsy caravan, the thin smoke curling from its funnel, the shafts swaying from side to side as the old horse plodded steadily on its journey into the unknown.

Already it was past him, already it was a dwindling figure on the road. And as he watched, knowing he could no longer move any more than he had ever done, he imagined that the tiny trap door at the back of the caravan opened and the raven hair and the shy white face of the gipsy girl appeared and looked back down the road. Perhaps she was looking back to him, perhaps her lips were speaking words, perhaps her eyes were beseeching and beckoning? He would never know.

He fell down upon his knees in the thick grass, still watching, still seeing the girl framed in the doorway like the vision of some saint. And as he watched the caravan disappear it seemed to him that with it went the whole retinue of his life's might-have-beens, as if the caravan was only the last of a long line of nomadic wandering things that had passed like golden silhouettes across his horizon – which had for a moment fused with his life, which might forever have become part of his life, but which he had let drain away between his outstretched fingers like sands of the desert.

And at last he knew himself to be drained of all life and all spirit, having no heart even for more failures.

Because there seemed no purpose or pattern at all, he did not return to the house. He walked slowly into the woods, and along the trampled pathway to where the caravan had stood, where he had watched it in those long delirium evenings.

He wandered about the clearing, walking round and round as if in some way to mark out its circle for his own. Then he came to the centre and crouched down before the ashes and the embers and the dried sticks. His eyes were dull, like stones that have endured too much rain; his shoulders sagged with their last burdens. Now what am I, he thought, now what am I any more than a beast of the wood, a beast of the jungle? Might I not as well belong here like the beast of the jungle, as in the square walls and carpeted floors of humanity? For am I not an outcast?

And he slowly bent and began blowing through pursed lips at the embers, blowing with deep slow puffs, as if in some deranged way expecting to bring life back to that which was dead.

*

In the afternoon Frances took the children with her into Bedruthan, first to do some necessary shopping (it seemed years since she had been into the town; certainly not since the evening they met Christine) then to have the great treat, tea at the oak-raftered Malt House Teashop.

Timothy wore his neat school-blazer and short trousers from which his thin brown legs emerged like shy young saplings. He had at last acceded to her request that he should wear his school cap, but it was perched so precariously on top of his wild curly hair that she kept having to restrain herself from putting a hand out to catch it every time he bent forward. On her other side Theresa walked with the gentle grace and grave dignity befitting a young lady. She looked sweet, Frances thought, in her little red jersey and the pleated skirt that Edith had knitted for her.

It was a brilliant sunlit day. It seemed almost as if they walked across golden sands when they went gaily down the high street, peering into first one shop and then another.

'Oh, Mummy, that dress – see that dress!' Theresa would call out, and as Frances obediently moved over she felt on her arm the grudging, bored weight of Timothy.

When they reached the Smith's bookshop, it was Timothy's warm, moist hand that pulled at her frantically, Theresa's turn to pout disconsolately. For Timothy was already passionately fond of his books.

Like his Uncle Raymond, she thought, and momentarily a frown crept over her face. She had not seen Raymond all that morning, not even at lunch. She supposed he had gone out in some burst of moodiness, perhaps walked over to Little Hurtwell, as he sometimes did. Yet she felt an odd uneasiness. She tried to convince herself that it was stupid to seek extra responsibility: Raymond's life was his own affair. But it was with difficulty that she banished his image from her mind.

In the bookshop they bought Timothy a book of illustrations of all the important types of railway trains. Theresa condescended to accept a book of pictures from the latest ballets. Sometime in the not too distant future, Frances had already promised she would take Theresa to London to see the ballet.

What fun they would have, she realised, buying herself a woman's magazine, an evening paper for Oliver. They would sit up in the gods, where all genuine ballet followers were to be found. Sometimes they would just sit in silence, listening to the remarks all around them – other times she would tell Theresa who was among the dancers, why they wore classical dresses for some dances and modern dresses for others. And other times she would be quiet and receptive and hear Theresa's soft voice struggling to express the inevitable flood of questions.

She warmed at the contemplation of the universality, youth growing up, the flowering out at the thought of her own rich part in it. She had a fleeting sense of pity for the women in life who never knew what it was to bear children, to mother them and watch them grow into reality.

'Can we go and have tea now, Mummy?' said Timothy determinedly.

'Well … I must just get some groceries, darling, then we'll go, I promise. It's only half past three you know.'

No fact could have obviously meant less to Timothy. In his small perky face was registered a single-minded anticipation of squishy cakes and toasted tea buns – preferably, no doubt, in that order. They crossed the road, and plunged into the exotic soft-carpeted depths of the teashop.

How nice it all is, she found herself thinking, as she returned the friendly nod of the manageress. How settled and pleasant – seeing across the tables a friend from the other side of the town – watching out of the window Mr Daker and his wife passing in their car ('Look, children, there's Mr Daker'), hearing Timothy's disparaging comment, 'Not much of a car, is it? Dowdy thing.'

How familiar, and yet how nice it all was. She frowned uneasily. She was thinking of the occasion two days ago when she had found Timothy looking up at her with a curious expression.

'Why, what is it, Timothy?' she had said. He had shaken his head and said, 'Oh, nothing, nothing.' And when she asked again he shook his head. It was some time before he looked away and mumbled, diffidently: 'Why didn't you drive in to Bedruthan with Daddy this morning?' And she knew he did not believe her vague response.

So now she looked at him a trifle anxiously, glad to see his mind fixed on something concrete.

'Nice cakes, Timothy?'

'Uhum. I've got a chocolate cream.'

'I can see that, darling. It's all over your mouth.'

A little later.

'Theresa, you're not eating.'

'Well, Mummy, I'm waiting to be passed the cakes. You said a lady always waited to be asked. Why doesn't Timothy ask me then?'

'You're quite right, darling. Timothy, what do you say?'

But she had to suppress a smile as Timothy carefully helped

himself to another eclair before lifting the plate and thrusting it almost under Theresa's nose.

At the end of the meal, smoking a cigarette, she smiled at them affectionately.

'We must come here again, soon.'

'Ooh, yes.' And their heads nodded, in violent agreement for once.

Then Timothy was leaning forward.

'Mummy, can we all come here – Daddy too?'

She flushed.

'Why, of course, darling. That's what I meant. All of us.'

And as she stubbed out the cigarette she was angry with herself for blushing. For she knew quite well that she meant it.

Later there was the exciting bus journey back, with Timothy walking about and collecting tickets, and exchanging pleasantries with the old countrymen and the housewives on their way back to lonely cottages.

And by the time they had walked up to the farm if they felt as tired as she did they would be more than ready for bed, she reflected.

That night she put them to bed early, giving them a hasty bath and then wrapping them up cosily in their blankets. She kissed them quickly, and then whispered good night and switched out the light. But when she had closed the door she stood there for a while, smiling, listening to their desultory conversation that would soon fade into the peace of their sleep.

She went across the landing to the top of the staircase, hesitating as she passed the little stairway up to Raymond's room. Again she felt that faint tremor of disturbance, the sense of something out of place. Should she go up to his room again? It was no use, he hadn't been there before when she went, and she was sure he hadn't come in. Still ... She called out: Raymond! Raymond! And once more, softly this time, like an echo dying away: Raymond!

There was no reply, only a faraway creak of a door blown by the wind, only a murmur of giggles from the children's room. She sighed and went down the stairs slowly, putting away the unease into the back of her mind.

She looked at the clock. Eight o'clock. Time to be getting some supper. She frowned, trying to remember. Was it tonight that Oliver went to the NFU branch meeting? She pressed her hand to her head, trying to remember. No wonder, she thought, when her head was nowadays a constant whirl of facts and fantasies. She had begun dreaming, dreams full of inexplicable journeys that reached no end but, if anything, seemed to halt, to expire, on the edge of some new, unimaginable happening. In one dream she was clad in a white sheet and laid out on an operating table, there was the bright glaring light of a hospital lamp falling upon her, hurting her eyes. Somewhere just above the light were faces, masked faces, and she knew by the eyes of one that it was Oliver. But when she cried out, desperately needing to be assured that she was not alone and lost to the talons of the surgeon, when she cried out Oliver, Oliver! – the eyes were blank and unrecognising, there was no one, nothing.

When she awoke she was alone in the bed: it was nearly eight o'clock and Oliver must have slipped away without waking her, to feed the chickens. For a long time she sat there staring across the room at the floral pattern of the wallpaper, willing herself not to be frightened, not to be stupid, not to scream.

She looked, now, down at her fist that had been pressed against her head, at the way it was clenched, at the tremble of the arm, and she remembered the angry shadows she saw in her eyes when she looked in the mirror that morning. Some conception of the ravages of emotional strain flickered deep inside her.

I *must* make sure whether it is the NFU evening, she thought. She went decisively into the dining-room, across to the writing desk where Oliver kept his correspondence.

As usual everything was neatly tucked away in drawers, so that she could not be sure quite where to look for the programme of the NFU meetings. She looked under the blotting paper, pulled open the side-drawers; one, two, three. She stopped as she was about to shut the third drawer, her eye caught by the name, printed in block letters on a slip of paper: Mark Hertz. It was in Oliver's writing, the name clipped at the front of a file of correspondence.

She hesitated, then slowly pulled the packet on to the desk. There were four or five letters, the top one on the notepaper of the County Agricultural Committee. She read, curiously.

> ... authorised to inform you that there has been an urgent request from the Forestry Commission for the services of any worker with previous experience of this work to join a new scheme of forestry in the Lake District. As I understand Mark Hertz, at present in your employ, falls into this category, I shall accordingly be recommending his name for transfer.

Under this letter was a copy of Oliver's reply. She read it slowly, with surprise, almost with a shock. It was one of Oliver's typical business letters, short sentences, blunt, precise. He wrote that Mark Hertz was one of the best workers he had ever had, and extremely valuable, and that if the Committee did not object he would rather he was not transferred. There was a further letter from the Committee trying to browbeat Oliver to fit into the preferred official procedure, but another rather peremptory reply seemed to have convinced them. In their last letter they agreed, as an exception, to sanction Mr Williams' request to be allowed to retain the services of Mark Hertz.

Frances put the letters down thoughtfully, still staring at them as she reclipped on top of them the scrap of paper with Mark's name. How easy it would have been for Oliver to accept this simple solution of Fate. No guilt would have attached to him, not even in acquiescing – for not to acquiesce would do him no good, might mean definite loss of influence for him. Committees did not like being flouted. And the temptation must have been ... considerable. She wondered how she would have acted. She hoped she would have done the same.

She put the letters back in the drawer. And as she pushed the drawer shut a vivid impression came upon her of Oliver sitting there with a blank sheet of paper before him and of Oliver writing in his firm, clear handwriting, closing the door of his escape.

All at once the vague feelings that had been hovering around her all that day crystallised into a tremendous tenderness towards Oliver. For she realised, with a shock, not that he understood – which was remarkable enough – but how much he understood. Not a word had been exchanged between them so much as to voice the idea, the thing that had to be understood; yet by this very action, symbolic in its way, he had unconsciously revealed the depth and reality of his love for her.

It ran through her like a flow of fresh water, this new knowledge of hers. It seemed to impart to her a new life and strength, to undo knots, to bring upon her a sweet calmness at a time of stress.

And all at once she wished she could see Oliver, wished she could equally well make him understand the nature of her own love for him. She felt that if just in that moment of illumination he could be there beside her, she could tell him, could connect with him, and he with her. But he was not there. Yet she was not unhappy, for she knew now that the love was there between them, unbreakable.

A moment later she found the programme. It was not the night of the meeting. Which meant, she supposed, that Oliver had been locking up and making a last round – perhaps looking at the rabbit traps.

But even so, it was late … She looked at her watch. Nine o'clock. Where had he got to? And where was Raymond? Out all day, it was strange … and strange to be so alone and without connection with them, no communication.

She walked into the hall and then, with a burst of relief, heard the back door opening, and the clip of Oliver's iron-tipped heels on the stone floor.

'Oh, Oliver – there you are. I was beginning to be worried. Darling, I –'

She stopped the words in mid-sentence, seeing Oliver framed in the doorway, a little dishevelled, seeing at once from the tautness, the slight pallor of his face, that something was amiss.

'Oliver – is anything the matter?'

'I don't know ...' He frowned. 'I've just had a message from Fred Parker, of the Rose and Crown. He sent his man Fuller over and I met him in the lane. He said that Raymond had been in there for a couple of hours drinking like a fish and getting tight, and talking wildly – well, he said, out of his hat. According to Fuller he got quite violent and rude to the others. In the end he went out in a huff, and Parker thought we ought to know as he doubted if he was in a fit state to find his way home.'

'Oh, Oliver!' The complex pattern of her own fantasies shattered before the crystallised image of her brother, before her intuitive knowledge of his torture and solitariness.

'Oliver, we must go and find him, help him home. It's a two mile walk across the woods and the fields. He's bound to get lost or something ... Oh, Oliver, I'm frightened.'

'There, there, don't get upset.' He put an arm clumsily around her. 'I'm going off at once now. I'll get Mark to look as well.'

'And I must come, too. Oh, but – the children.'

'No, you mustn't come, you can't leave them. Besides, if Raymond is drunk, he's easier dealt with by a man than a woman.' Oliver began putting on a yellow cape over his overcoat. 'It's pouring with rain, too. A fine night to go looking for a drunk in the dark!'

He went to the back door, Frances following with her hands pressed together.

'Do be careful.'

'I will. You keep a look out. He may miss us and come here. I should have some hot coffee or something.'

Oliver disappeared into the yard. She listened to his footsteps crossing until she could hear no more, thought of him walking into the swish of the rain, across to Mark's hut. Mark ... and Oliver. Oliver. Mark.

With an effort she shut the door against the rising strength of the windstrewn rain.

*

Raymond turned off the lane and picked his way painfully up the bank of the reservoir. The day had vanished behind him into a grey mist, his mind had shrunk in its contemplations until it focused only upon the idea of Mark and his enormous guilt – the stranger who had riven open his life and Frances' life and Oliver's life. Mark, the German and the enemy, the instigator of the whole tortured byway of his life's journey.

All day long he had mooned about the woods, peering behind trees and suddenly darting among the foliage, half convinced of some enemy lurking there, perhaps Mark dogging his footsteps like an accusation from the past. In the public house he bought four whiskies in a row and drank them neat, then he began talking to himself in a voice that rose louder and louder, like the wail of some immense funeral ceremony that had been set into motion. He was hardly aware that his voice became a high-pitched scream, nor of the gibberish of dreams and words that he poured out, but he felt them looking, felt the faces gathering round him like unwanted sentinels.

It was as much a theatrical gesture as any real desire that prompted him to sweep the glasses off the table into little pieces and fling out of the pub in such a spate of violent rage that no one dared to stop him. But once outside he became possessed with a premonition that, as always, dragged him, foot by foot towards the reservoir – as if it was now an acknowledged part of his purpose that whatever it was, it should be executed at the scene of the reservoir. He walked shamblingly, as a man might do who had abdicated from the struggle to direct his life and had given himself up into the stream of some secret motivation.

He was not surprised when he saw the light flickering at the far end of the towpath. He knew that it would be Mark. It was all part of the pattern of this rain-soaked night, part of the sequence of events that must be unfolded in this cover of darkness. He even, in a calmer moment, found time to contemplate himself as some lonely knight embarking on the slaying of the dragon – the German dragon.

His mind, in the cloak of wet night, raced back to the other fields, the flooded fields in France, the barking night guns, the flickering sky, the rumble-rumble on the horizon of the undeterrable enemy. There were the machine-guns and the line of hidden killers, and there was somewhere a Travers – but this time there would be no cringing, frightened figure running back into the darkness.

As the light came nearer he crouched a little way down the side of the bank, pressing himself into the grass. He had the clear impression of these moments as the prelude to an immense gesture, a symbol, that would somehow obviate everything, would reinstate him and his life across all the wasted years. He thought about this with a great glow of satisfaction, and with it thought of the imponderable purposes of the action he would take – not only upon his life, but upon Frances, and Oliver, the children, the farm – an entity of people and processes. It even began to seem to him, shrouded in the darkness, drowned in the wind and the rain, pressed into the beating heart of the earth, that perhaps an entire world might now be held within the clenched curve of his two hands.

And when Mark appeared above, swinging a small hurricane lantern, Raymond sprang at him with an inhuman velocity and strength, smashing his two fists at the shadowy face, throwing all the weight of his body at the hated figure.

It was more than enough to throw the unsuspecting Mark off his balance, to hurl him sideways into the shocking space beyond the parapet – down to the wide wet gleam of the reservoir water.

It happened in a few seconds. There was the swift hiss of movement, the tumbling body, the untidy splashing. Raymond stood, rooted, on the towpath, a body wanting to tremble all over that was yet frozen into a statue.

Then Mark cried out:

'I can't swim! I can't swim!'

For Raymond the voice was something new, something entirely original, the first image of humanity reaching out to him from the future to a past that had suddenly dissolved. As if in the moment of his physical action, in the ferocity of his attack, was concentrated a lifetime of frustration and hatred and hopelessness; as if all had been packed like a compressed force into his two hands, had been flung and exhausted in the same moment. Leaving him naked and unprotected, stripped to the spirit of himself.

In the next moment, consciously and without hesitation, he dived in the water.

Feeling with his hands through the water, he got hold of Mark's coat, heavy and damp.

'It's all right. I've got you. Can you hear me?'

He heard a faint groan of assent.

'Hang on, then.'

He realised, with a faint shiver of surprise, that the wind and rain had created a strong current, that already they were being blown out to the centre.

'Hold tight!'

Clinging to Mark's shoulder with one hand he attempted to strike out, pushing with his feet, trying to make strokes with his free hand. But it was patently no use. He could feel, could see by looking at the bank, that they were slowly and inexorably being swept outwards. And the reservoir was a huge one. If he couldn't get to the bank now he never would. He was not a very good swimmer himself. The practicalities of the matter flashed through his mind like a film.

Then he remembered, grasping at the idea; a little way further down there was a narrow wooden pier stretching out, from which the old villagers used to come and do their fishing. He remembered that there were rows of strong steel bars – if he was lucky, he might be able to grasp at some of the scaffolding.

He brushed the water out of his eyes, trod water and peered ahead. It was like being a part of a fantasy world of water, the rain sheeting down, the reservoir water whipped up into angry waves by the wind. Any other time, he reflected, he would have been terrified. But now the urgency of the position, the weight upon his arm, seemed to take possession of all his emotional strength.

Suddenly the tip of the pier loomed ahead of him. He gritted his teeth. Yes, with luck they would float at it – with luck, with luck and deliberation. Making a tremendous effort he kicked and stroked his way against the tide, trying to reach a few feet nearer to the shore. They were almost upon the pier now. He saw the steel scaffolding rising up in the darkness, the water all around.

'Can you hear me?' he cried wildly. 'We've got to get on to this pier. Now when I cry out, you must make an effort. You must try to get a grip.'

He never knew whether Mark heard him or not. The next second a wave carried them up to the very end section. They bumped against the steel rafter with an agonising force. He felt, at once, the crunching of shattered bones and muscle. The pain shot through him like a fire through dry bush; unbearable, unbelievable. Yet for a moment longer he clung to his purpose. With a superhuman effort he pushed Mark's unresisting body upwards. 'Get a grip. For God's sake get a grip!'

Somehow, he supposed instinctively, he felt Mark's hands grip on to the top of the steel pole, felt the weight of Mark's body on himself slacken. He gave a last tremendous shove, and he realised that the German had got a grip and was now lying across the floor of the pier – safe.

And then he became aware of himself. Something terrible had happened, he knew. His two legs had been wedged between the steel girders. A wave had spun him round – breaking, breaking, twisting him beyond endurance. He felt his head spinning, strange blood streams coursing through him, a band of pain across his back …

Painfully he wrapped his hands around the bottom of the girder. It was sufficient to hold his head above water, but he could move no more; he must stay there and endure each battering, spitting wave. Stay there through the long dark night until by some miracle someone else came by, or until Mark recovered himself.

'Mark!' he cried. 'Mark!'

But there was no reply. Mark's figure lay spreadeagled like a dreamer lost into a great sleep.

So he cried out no more. He clung to the steel post with a

ferocious strength, as if clinging to something that was suddenly precious, and the strength came to him because it was the dark pit and he was going to pass through it if it lasted for an eternity – because he willed himself that he would not be lost into it.

They were both there in their separate and painful worlds an hour later, when Oliver found them in the firm beam of his torch.

X

The children appeared on the lawn as Mark was in the middle of playing a rippling Brahms sonata that seemed to have captured all the trill and whirling of a dancing wind among the tree tops. And indeed, it seemed almost as if they were two wind-blown fairies summoned by his playing, Theresa in her billowing blue summer frock and Timothy in his yellow swim-suit, the two of them pirouetting to the sound of the piano.

He played on, gaily, to the end, and then watched their two flushed, excited faces loom against the window panes, hot breaths throwing up the ghostly circles of mist. Two snub red noses pressed against the glass that was the wall between their world and his. Too many walls, he thought savagely; there was always, at the least, a glass wall.

'Can we come and listen, Mark?'

'We won't be a nuisance, promise.'

'Yes, we'll be quiet as mice.'

He opened the French windows wide, letting the sun and the warm afternoon air into the dusty atmosphere of the library.

'But, of course. You will be an audience. I shall be honoured.'

He smiled at them gravely, the smile a striking contrast to the formidable bandage that he still wore round his head where it had been lacerated against the pier that night a week ago. But otherwise he was none the worse.

'It was nice music, was it not?' he said. 'I saw it made you dance.'

Theresa's eyes sparkled at him. She had been the ballerina,

the soloist, the great Pavlova – he read it all in those joyous, innocent eyes.

'Play some more like that, then I will dance in here.'

'Very well.' He poised his hands. 'But you will be careful – the furniture?'

'Yes, of course I will. Oh, do play, please.'

So he played one of the Hungarian waltzes, softly, while the child waltzed gracefully around the long dark library, passing in and out of the chairs and the little tables, with a natural grace that was exquisite to observe. She is a dancer, a born dancer, he thought, and smiled with pleasure to see in the future a triumphant fulfilment of Frances' dreams. A beautiful and a great dancer, he thought, and he felt an exhilaration enter into him and through him into the music, and through the music into Theresa, so that for a few moments the music and the dancing were uplifted and rarefied, an achievement of purity. It was as if the music was not played by the two hands of Mark Hertz but was the music of all mankind, a million voices swelling and ebbing like the sea; as if it was not Theresa, but all childhood that danced; the voice of mankind and the beauty of childhood, a wonder of creation transcending the realities and the materials and the limitations of ordinary life.

When he stopped he felt the exhilaration still tingling in his fingertips, and he said impulsively:

'For that, thank you, little Theresa. You danced like an angel.'

'Oh, more, Mark – can we have more?'

But Timothy looked glum.

'She's always dancing and dancing. Can't you play some music where she doesn't dance?'

Mark laughed.

'That would be hard indeed, Timothy. But I tell you what. You will sit here beside me – or no, look, I will lift you up and you can sit on top of the piano like that, then you can watch me play and Theresa dancing. Is that good?'

And with Timothy sitting proudly at the highest vantage point, Mark played and Theresa danced and mimed and pirouetted, while the brilliant afternoon sun sank lower and flooded the library like some supernatural stage.

When even Theresa was exhausted and sank puffing into a chair, Mark stopped playing. He smiled at Timothy, who was looking down at him intently.

'My, your fingers must be very clever,' said Timothy. 'Sometimes I couldn't see them at all.'

'It is only practice.'

'An' did you have to practise a lot?'

'Of course he did, silly,' explained Theresa. 'Like I have to practise my dancing. You'd never be any good, you never practise at anything.'

Mark lifted Timothy gently down to the seat.

'Yes, quite a lot of practice.' He held one of his hands in front of Timothy. 'You see, at first the fingers are slow and clumsy. Besides, they do not know what to do, which notes to play.'

'And did you have music sheets with little black dots on them? Do they have those in Germany, too?'

'Oh, yes. For years and years I used to sit in front of music sheets and play and play. Sometimes four or five hours every day.'

'Coo! Didn't you get tired?'

'Quite a lot. But you see I wanted to be a good pianist, so I was determined to work hard.'

'And did you go and play in front of a lot of people?'

'Oh, yes. Many times.'

'That must have been exciting,' said Timothy thoughtfully. 'Do people like music in Germany then?'

Mark put his fingers out upon the keys, gently pressing the echo of a chord.

'Yes, Timothy. Very much.'

'More than the people in England?'

'Well, I couldn't tell you that. Most people like music.'

Timothy pondered.

'And is the music in Germany the same as in England, then?'

'Well, in a way – yes. People in England are very fond of German music. Just like people in Germany are very fond of

English poetry and plays – like Shakespeare. I remember seeing a Shakespeare festival at Nuremberg when I was a little boy not much older than you. Thousands of people came to see it.'

'Coo!' said Theresa from her chair. 'I wish I'd been there.'

'Well,' said Timothy after a portentous pause, 'if the people in Germany like English poetry and the people in England like German music, why do they have to have wars with each other?'

'I don't know, Timothy,' said Mark. 'I've never known.'

'Uncle Raymond says wars are a mistake, too. And Oliver. If everyone thinks they're a mistake how can there be a war again?'

'Silly!' said Theresa. 'How do you know what people in Germany think? Have you been there?'

'No-o,' admitted Timothy doubtfully. He looked up at Mark. 'Do you think people in Germany want another war?'

'No, no. Of course they don't. Only a few perhaps … Some here and there, who don't understand.'

'Oh,' said Timothy. 'Then hadn't you better go and tell them not to be silly?'

Mark looked at the round child-face, the unshadowed eyes that reflected all the sweet innocence and goodness that existed, always, in every human being. In one of those rare moments of complete clarity, he saw how irrevocable was his purpose and his destiny. And he no longer hated and dreaded the crumpled letter in his pocket, the terse official instructions, the memorandum that must annihilate a happiness.

'Of course,' he said. He began speaking rapidly and with emotion. 'Of course, you are right, Timothy. That is just what I am going to do.'

Beckoning Theresa to come and sit by him on the wide stool, he put an arm round them each.

'I am going back to Germany, and wherever I go I shall play music, like we've been playing now. Gay and happy music, sometimes serious music, too – but above all music that contains love and truth and beauty, music that is universal and that means something everywhere. Because you see, Timothy and Theresa, music is the one language that is spoken all over the world, it is the one way in which you can unite people and give them warmth and peace and understanding ... You probably don't quite know what I'm talking about, but you will one day. Other men try to do the same sort of thing with books, with plays, with films. It is all good, everything is good that breaks down the accursed barriers and iron walls. I am not a good speaker, perhaps I do not know the right words even – but I can speak through music. I know I can give pleasure and comfort to people – and because I know that, it is my duty to do so for ever and ever, as long as I am able to, as long as I live. That is the duty of all artists ... You will know that, Theresa, one day when you become a great dancer.'

He smiled.

'Who knows, Theresa, one day perhaps I shall play for you and you will dance before an audience of kings and princesses and heaven knows what! But never any better than this afternoon.'

'Are you going away, Mark?' said Timothy wonderingly, his eyes rounding as they tried to visualise this immense expedition on which Mark would have to set out, across seas and mountains and rivers and cities, to reach the mystic land of Germany.

'Yes,' said Mark sadly. 'In a very short time.'

Suddenly there was a hush, an imperceptible pause, and in that pause the three of them were instinctively impelled to turn and see, framed in the doorway which she had just opened, Frances. She looked fresh and lovely, like the corn, in a bright yellow dress, her hair tumbling round her shoulders, bathed in the rich light of the sun streaming through the French windows. But the gold of her face was a false and drained colour.

For, across the distance already yawning between them, her seeking eyes found Mark's and read in them the confirmation of what she had heard – read in them the beginning and the sweet middle and now the sad end of their story – saw in them the welling of hidden tears to measure her own.

'Yes,' he said to her. 'The letter has come. I have to report – tomorrow.'

And as, in a swift movement, she shepherded the children out of the library and into the kitchen for their tea, he sat where he was, his hands gentle and sleeping on the piano keys, saying to himself as if he still could not quite believe it.

'Tomorrow.'

When she came in and shut the door behind her and laid her head back against it looking across the void at him, when she looked at him with the tears coming like summer rain, slow and remorseless, he could only whisper: 'So little time, so little time.'

But as they ran to each other in a moment of unity, he cried, bravely:

'Yet it has been all the time in the world. An eternity! Hasn't it?'

And she nodded.

*

On that inevitable morning, while black horsemen still rode across the grey-gold dawn, Raymond awoke from a light sleep at the crunch of steps on the gravel: looked out of the window and saw the grey shape that was Mark crossing the yard to the white-barred gate and the long journey.

He thought to himself, curiously, he's going away early, before anyone's awake, so that there shall be no shock and no pain of the obvious farewell. And he watched with an ache of pity as Mark climbed the gate, shouldered his pack, took a quick backward look and then marched steadily down the muddy lane. The understanding of Mark's effort, heightened within him by his own experience, was increased by the sheer physical aspect – the solitary figure walking into the lonely morning, not going to anyone, not with the waiting welcome of family or lover at the end of the journey, only going to somewhere, disappearing into a nothingness out of which, once more, he must build his own world. And he would; for in the effort of departure was the foundation of the future.

Arrival and departure, was that not the spiral track on which the universe travelled? And he thought, with his new wisdom: for Mark it is the time of departure, for me the time of arrival.

He was sitting in bed, propped up by a great heap of cushions, the two legs that stretched in front of him under the white coverlet were completely encased in plaster-of-Paris. They had each been broken by the constant crushing against the pier scaffolding. There was a strong possibility that the spine was affected, that he might never walk again. And there was also the slender hope that he might – in some years' time.

He was a prisoner in a box called a room. Chained to his bed, as a manacled man to the wall of his cell. Able to look at the world, as any chained prisoner, only through the four-sided aperture of a window. Without even the humblest prisoner's privilege of pacing his precious steps up and down the tiny cell floor.

And yet at last he was happy and he was free.

All my life, he thought, staring out of the window and watching the slow wonder of a new day unfolding, the mist lifting and the sunshine licking awake the flowers and the trees, the wandering animals stretching themselves into life again – all my life I have been moving backwards. He remembered, though he supposed it had begun longer ago than that, the time of his early schooldays, the flinching from the crowd and the first turning into the self. And ever since then, the retreat, step by step, delusion by delusion, the withdrawal that was denial, the horrific, tortuous path of escape from the world into – emptiness.

And once embarked upon such a journey, he now realised, there could be no hesitation, no stepping off at a half-way stage. For it was a downward journey and there was the momentum that gathered speed and smashed through all the puny fragmentary scaffoldings and make-shift patchings, that dragged you down and down and down with a frightening intensity, down towards the barren pit.

He saw now, in the fantasy mirror of the window-panes, with the sunshine glinting upon them, the ghost of himself, the shroud and the skeleton that had hurtled towards its oblivion; the fugitive from schooldays, the fugitive from the strange outer world, the fugitive from the Germans, the fugitive from the truth – the ghost that could only at last retreat, that could not take a single step forward, not even in the shadows of a wood lit up by the reality of a beautiful girl. Retreat and retreat and retreat, escape and escape and escape. Until everything was reduced to a room with four walls; until, like some harassed animal, he had withdrawn into his last lair, some black cavern in the mountain, only to find it an illusion and the greatest horror of all.

He smiled faintly, not without pride. He was in that same room, now, the same four walls and the same furniture – the same bed, except that it had been moved to the window so that he could look out without stirring from his confined position.

And yet it was quite a different room.

The only possible end to his retreat, to all retreats and wild escapes, was a crash, some enormous violence. It had come for him that night, lost in the dark rain, when he hurled not only himself but the pent-up frustration of his whole life at the symbolic figure of Mark. It was as if the very fact of the action claimed for him a moment of decision, an imperceptible pause in which he became like a man poised upon the edge of precipice … to have fallen over which would have been the final annihilation.

But he had made the gesture, he had clutched the over-hanging ledge. When without thinking he dived in to save Mark it was the act of redemption, and the symbol of recovery.

It was strange, he thought, fingering at the window-pane which his breath had covered with a faint film of moisture – strange into what simple sequences and patterns the processes of existence conformed. It was as simple as if, like now, he wiped the window-pane clear and the face he saw reflected was a new, somehow a more familiar face. As if each time he blew gently on the pane and then wiped, the face grew more familiar – as if each time he rubbed the mirror he saw not only a different face of his own, but a different aspect of mankind.

And that this was not the occasion of despair, but of wonder. For nothing was final and everything contained in itself its opposite – through disease was health, beyond courage lay fear, in ignorance was understanding, out of strength grew weakness, underneath despair lay hope – in death even there could be life.

And so, he reflected, gently opening the window and letting in the rush of the fresh morning air of a new day, and so one could make a beginning. One could arrive at an understanding: that *was* the beginning.

The beginning was simple that life was made not to be measured but to be accepted. If you accepted, everything, then the whole of life was open to you, exhilarating, exciting, joyous, tremendous an inexhaustible adventure.

And for such an adventure, he thought, with a surprised contentment that he could still hardly believe – for such an adventure, he thought, staring placidly at the cool white pattern of the ceiling, itself as flooded with potential riches as the faraway waters of the reservoir – for such an adventure it does not matter in the least whether one has two legs or four, or none of all.

As long as one has a heart and a head.

'So you see, Frances,' he said cheerfully, when Frances brought in his cup of tea, when she placed it neatly on his lap and drew the curtains wide, sniffing at the radiant air, ' "my accident", as you persist in calling it, is probably the best thing that could have happened to me.

'Why,' he said, waving his arm around, 'why, look at my good fortune. A comfortable position, a loved one to wait on me, a look out of my window upon a whole exciting world, a stream of books to bring before me not one but hundreds of other worlds ... Last of all, as you –' he took her arm in an impulsive loving grip – 'as you alone may understand, Frances, I have the greatest world of all, that I have never before been able to explore without wreckage and impasse.

'A sheet of blank paper,' he said thoughtfully, holding it up in front of him, letting the sunshine impart to it strange and lovely patterns, shadows and the implications of innumerable hidden fantasies.

On that paper, at last, he knew he could write himself into being, could find the words and meanings, the images of truth, that had previously seemed to escape out of his head like slippery, scaly fishes.

'Listen, Frances,' he said eagerly, pushing the tray aside.

'This is a story I wrote last night. It seemed to pour out of me. I don't know yet whether it's good or not. But I can't help feeling it's perhaps the best.'

He cleared his throat.

'It's called "The Seeker", and it's about a man who left his home to roam the world in a search for happiness. And how wherever he searched he was disappointed until one day he looked into a mirror ...'

He read it aloud, in his deep voice, while the morning poured in through the window and the chattering of awakened birds swelled into music. Frances knew then that it was the best thing he had written, and that he had found himself.

*

'When I was a little boy on my father's arm I used to think only in terms of size. I wanted to ride always the biggest of the horses, the one called "Prince". My favourite field was the biggest one, where you could go out with a plough and get lost all day and still not come to the end of the work. I suppose somehow it was a sort of challenge.'

Oliver shifted restlessly in the driving seat of the stationary Lagonda, parked in the sunshine on the top of a hill.

'I remember how impressed I was to meet a friend of my father, another farmer, who worked not one but three separate farms. And how ever after that my father sank a little in my estimation because he only worked a mere forty-five acres while his friend Jim Wilson worked about two hundred acres. Silly, wasn't it? And yet it was very easy to think like that ... to go on thinking like that.'

He pointed through the windscreen to the wide lowland stretching below them, an enormous canvas of neat cultivated fields, here and there a clump of trees, the reservoir, a stately old mansion, the streaky line of smoke left by an express train to Plymouth.

'When we first came here I used often to come and stand on this hill. I used to rather fancy myself as a king looking over his domain. It wasn't entirely a joke, either. I would look down there to our farm and think, it's very nice, and I'll get that going first. Then, yes, I'll buy up the land adjoining and cultivate that. And *then*, more land. And more; I really used to think, sometimes, that perhaps one day I'd farm the whole plain.'

He laughed.

'Sounds crazy, doesn't it? Well, it was in a way. A sort of obsession. It was all I really thought about – it became a mania, like a poison eating into one.'

He glanced quickly at Frances' bent head and then away again.

'Oh, yes, it took me quite a long time to see what was wrong. And of course, like all drug addicts, self-poisoners, I grew cunning. I found reasons, excuses to persuade myself why it was absolutely essential to go on and on, to become bigger and bigger. I even used to tell myself I had to work harder and harder for the sake of you – for my family's sake.' He frowned. 'But not often – not half often enough.'

'It was so simple. I had bought the farm, I had bought you – those two things were tucked away, safely acquired. My enthusiasm turned towards new fields, new possessions. I didn't even take a lesson from the elementary experience with my own land – that to neglect it is a bad investment.'

And now he could feel her crying, her tiny curved body shaking in slow ebbs. He put his arm round her gently as if to absorb the impact of each sob.

'Oh!' he cried suddenly, 'I was so stupid. It is I, *I* who am to blame – *I* who am guilty of causing you suffering, if anyone is.'

She blinked away the tears, fingering at the dark knob of the gear lever.

'But now you'll hate me – you'll always feel cheated, I know you will. And it's so silly,' she added with a flash of spirit. 'Because if you only knew –'

He raised his hand and turned her face gently towards him.

'But Frances, if you'll only let me say what I was going to – after all, damn it, I've been rehearsing it for days!' he said with a grin, and in that moment of humour sweeping away the false barricades. He took her hand and held it tight, as if he would never let it go again.

'I suppose a man is less wise than a woman ... he always thinks in terms of water-tight compartments. Or he does until he learns better. That's how it was with me. I loved you, you loved me, we were married, we had children – there was a neat little compartment.'

He hesitated.

'It never struck me that it could be opened, or perhaps widened. When I found out – about Mark – it was terrible.'

He felt her crying again, and drew her head against the deep folds of his overcoat.

'Don't cry, Frances. Please don't.'

'I can't help it. And yet – you must know – I love you very, very deeply.'

'But, yes, I do!'

And he almost laughed in exultation at the glory of his new senses, of his capacity for seeing at last beyond the horizons that had confined him.

'I do, really. Because – oh, how can I put it clearly? Because I see now that love can't be put into water-tight compartments – because there's no end to it. That's what I'm trying to get at. At first I felt suicidal, finished. I assumed that our love was gone, transferred as you might say.

'Now I know that to be a selfish viewpoint, and a limited one. Your loving Mark hasn't altered our love – I can see that now. It has enriched you, and it has given Mark back his life ... and it has helped me to understand a simple fact.

'For the truth is, simply, that in all of us there is an infinite capacity for love, and the more we express it the better for us and the world.'

And he pulled his arms tighter around her, feeling in that moment the sense of her passing into his being again; a return and a renewal.

*

Later they drove back to the farm. It was the first day of the potato-picking. They left the car by the gate and walked across to the long field, bathed in the brilliant afternoon sun. The pickers were strung out in two lines, waiting while the squat blue tractor chugged up and down, the plough behind it throwing up the potatoes to be gathered by the pickers into the waiting baskets and sacks. Everyone was there, men and women from the village, three girl students in bright green jerseys, Edith with her thick grey hair tucked up in a home-made bandeau – last and not least, Timothy and Theresa, burrowing and jumping about like startled rabbits. Without another word Frances and Oliver picked up a sack and joined the line of workers. Soon they were one with them in the steady rhythm of the potato-picking, the sun winking on the white shirts of the men and the coloured dresses of the women, the blue tractor steadily narrowing the green sea of potato-plants into a pathetic miniature of the greater, enormous blue sea of a sky that filled the world above.

Watching from his open window Raymond thought he had never seen a more beautiful sight, and knew it was a profound moment of peace and fulfilment. He picked up his pen and began writing.